FLOW OVERRIDE

A PIPER CADENCE THRILLER

FLOW
BOOK 1

JACE STROUD

VLS
PUBLISHING

To Carrie, who read every page like it mattered. You reminded me why writing is worth it.

As I put it, to paraphrase another: The ethics laws do not let us tap out the truth in Morse code.

RON WYDEN

$\bullet = dot$
$— = dash$

ONE

The wipers kept up their thump-thump-thump, all chipper, doing their best to make Piper's night less miserable. It wasn't working. She sat in the driver's seat two houses down, engine off, counting the thumps in her head. She'd gotten to twenty-three when a message appeared in her overlay, making her lose count. Rourke's voice played in her head, rough as always, but tonight it was worse. Like he'd swallowed a handful of gravel and chased it with dread, "It's a bad one, Cadence. The Moreau house... The weirdest yet."

That was it. No protocol. No Detective. Just the facts, shoved into her brain, like she had any choice but to listen.

Rain dripped in fat, uneven splats from the top of the windshield. Each one traced its own path until the wipers swept through and smeared the police lights into shaky arcs of red and blue. The crime scene tape around the Moreau house bounced when large raindrops hit it. People probably referred to it as a boundary, but it looked more like a stage curtain. Whatever waited inside, she was going to have to put on a show for it.

She pressed her thumb against the frayed edge of her blazer

cuff and started picking at it. Her AI Therapist called the habit adaptive tactile regulation. She called it fidgeting. That word felt a lot more honest than anything clinical ever could.

A shadow moved off to the side of the porch. Someone in a rain shell, who looked like a uniform, ducked under the awning and stood just out of the light. She needed to get out. She knew she should get out. Instead, she stared at the house, trying to spot something, anything, some variable or data point that would let her stall, even for a minute, before she had to go inside and deal with things.

If Rossi were here, he'd do the whole rookie-not-ready routine —maybe crack a joke about corpses, then give her that look and say the best way to beat nerves was to picture the crime scene naked. It never made sense, but he'd always go first and let her follow. That was the trick. She'd never figured out how to lead.

But Rossi wasn't here. He was downtown now, doing Interpersonal Liaison, which was a nicer way of saying he spent his time babysitting politicians and teaching their staff how not to screw up a statement. She was alone. Only backup was Rourke, who sounded half a step from puking on his shoes.

Her hand froze on the blazer. She got annoyed at herself for picking at it and made herself send a message back. She subvocalized, "Copy, Rourke. Visual perimeter check in progress. ETA one minute."

What a dumb lie. There wasn't any perimeter. She just needed sixty seconds to remember how to breathe like a normal human.

Alright. Tools, then.

She subvocalized, "AI Therapist. Run the Flow app."

A chime. The AI Therapist's voice was the same as always, that default soothing tone. "*Activating Flow's breathing routine, Detective Cadence.*" Then a new voice took over, specifically designed for

Flow: slow, male, and deliberately calm. "*Please center your atten-tion on the visualization provided.*"

A splash of blue-green light popped up in her field of vision, hovering right where the dash met the windshield. It was a simple looping mandala, swelling and shrinking, totally in sync with her breathing. Breathe in, the mandala got bigger. Exhale, smaller. This was supposed to make her feel less like she was about to crawl out of her skin. Lower her alarms. Fix her, basically.

It never quite worked. But sometimes it took the edge off.

This time, her vision tunneled. Dashboard lights sharpened, and the rain outside got aggressive, every single drop exploding against the car like a personal landmine. The cop lights through the window stopped being blurry streaks and turned into stabbing pins of color, poking straight through her. She tried to keep her breathing matched up with the mandala, but every inhale felt like dragging glass across her lungs.

"Cancel Flow," she subvocalized.

"*Flow cancellation confirmed,*" the AI said, calm as ever, even though her vision was sparking at the edges.

It was only a little over a week since she installed the Flow add-on to her AI Therapist, but sometimes it made things shittier. Like she was wading through fog, and the world left a bruise after. She logged the side effects and let herself slouch down in the seat for a second.

There was supposed to be no shame in needing help. That's what the city trainings said, the ones with the giant posters of perfect, diverse officers with big smiles and their arms around each other. But if she showed up at the scene like this—fogged—they'd red-flag her for a wellness audit before she even crossed the tape.

The fog faded, but didn't go away completely. She'd have to fake it.

She let her breath out slowly, counted the seconds. One. Two. Three. It didn't help, but it would have to do.

There was another ping in her overlay, but this time it was a text message, floating just above the rain-slicked curb.

Ready?

She glanced up. Rourke stood under a streetlight, barely more than a silhouette in the downpour; the shadows from his hood hid his face, but it didn't matter. She already knew the look he wore: chin tucked down, avoiding eye contact.

Most people forgot what he was. It helped that he got cold like everyone else, hated audits, and chewed aspirin for migraines. The synthetic stuff was just paperwork buried in a medical file. Right now, though, watching him stand there, so perfectly, humanly hesitant, she knew what she had to do. Take the lead.

She always did.

She flicked the wipers off and popped the car door. Rain slapped her neck, icy and mean, racing under her collar and seeping down her back.

She didn't even shiver.

Instead, she straightened up, rolled her shoulders, and put on her practiced media face. The look she'd trained for, the one the city liked best, smooth and open and not a hint of what she was really thinking.

As she passed Rourke without a glance, she could picture exactly how he would walk behind her—two steps back, careful, respectful, like he was worried she'd turn on him if he got too close.

They closed in on the Moreau house. The police tape flapped in the wind, sad and pointless, but she ducked under it anyway. Rules were rules.

Her shoes hit the wet cement path that led to the house, and she heard Rourke, this time in real life, his voice weirdly raw. "They said it's bad, but I didn't think—" He clammed up. Tried again. "You ready?"

What was she supposed to say? The easy answer. The one Rossi would've tossed out with a wink and a dumb joke.

Instead, she told the truth.

"No," she said, and pushed the door open.

TWO

The first thing Piper noticed was the heat, which was hotter inside the Moreau place than outside. The second thing was the smell—old fruit, sticky sweet, turning to rot. Under that, a whiff of metal, familiar and sharp: blood. She stopped just past the front door, not moving farther yet. Voices carried from the kitchen, but she tuned them out and let her overlay map the living room.

Couch. Armchair, navy fabric. Glass coffee table, almond-shaped lamp, all normal living room items. Everywhere else were books. Hundreds. Built-in shelves, books standing side by side, books stacked on top of each other, some with cracked spines, some fresh as the day they were printed. At the very bottom, a row of kids' books—picture books for little hands, chapter books for slightly bigger ones.

That made sense, in a way, because three feet from the coffee table, there was a brown stain splashed across the cream carpet. Blood. Thick and half-dried now. No drag marks, no blood smeared on the girl's pajamas with bright green frogs, so the kid had just dropped right there. No struggle, and none of the horror you sometimes saw. Small favor. It meant she hadn't seen it coming.

The mother was slouched sideways in the armchair, head tipped like she'd dozed off mid-program. Piper had seen this before: a tidy, star-shaped hole above the ear; a mist of blood on the window behind. No exit wound. Low-caliber, or the round was still inside the skull. Clean, for what it was.

She checked the girl again. Maybe eight years old. Messy braid. Her face was peaceful except for the mess where her right eye should have been. Piper noticed a little crust at one nostril, but nothing else.

Rourke came up behind her and said, "Jesus."

"Yeah." Piper stared into the kid's face. What had she seen last? Her toy? A flicker from the TV? Her mom? Did it matter?

Evidence tags dotted the carpet—yellow cards lined up like a funeral procession. She let her overlay fill them in: AUTOTAG 1, FIBERS; AUTOTAG 2, BLOOD DROPLET; AUTOTAG 3, FIREARM. She cut off the rest. Too much. Her head still throbbed from the fog episode earlier, and random data made it worse. She preferred her own eyes anyway.

There was a shell casing under the coffee table, glinting in the dust.

She pointed. "Semi-auto, from the casing." She turned toward the window. "No forced entry, which means it's not a break-in. Status on the ex?"

Rourke had it ready. "Deadbeat. Gone six years, no contact after the last custody fight. Never licensed a gun. Moved north."

She scanned the rest of the room. Every surface had something personal: a chewed plastic dinosaur on the table, an art project with blobs of blue glue, a coffee mug that read "Knowledge is Power." It all clashed with the violence on the carpet.

"Was the mom on anything?" Piper asked.

Rourke shook his head. "Nothing prescribed. Her AI Therapist flagged mild anxiety, but no drugs, no history of substance use."

The sound that left her was a tired expulsion of air, too rough for a sigh but too soft for a grunt. "Any record of violence?"

"None. Anna Moreau's background is—" He paused, probably scrolling in his overlay. "—cleaner than mine."

Piper stepped closer to the mother. The dead didn't lie, which was why she liked working homicide. She bent down and looked at the woman's hands. Forensic residue painted little clouds of gunpowder. The mother had definitely fired the gun.

Across the room, the wall shelf had framed photos of the two of them. Usual stuff: a city park, a little girl with missing front teeth, Anna Moreau holding a poster at a rally. For a second, the photo went blurry, a side effect of the fog, but Piper blinked, and the image snapped back. Anna, wearing an orange vest with a "Gun Sense Now" banner.

"She was a gun-control advocate," Piper said, her eyes fixed on the photo.

"Looks like it," Rourke said.

She glanced at the body again. "Then where'd she get the gun?"

Rourke shrugged. "It could be a family piece, but we will know soon. They're running the trace."

On the end table beside Anna was a stack of books. On top was a fat hardcover. Even before she read the title, she knew the kind of book: "Nonviolence: The Only Way Forward."

The book was open to a dog-eared page. A sticky note poked out, "coffee, milk, toilet paper." Underneath, scrawled in crayon, "I lov Mom."

She closed her eyes. The easy theory, sad mom, has a break, then tragedy, was too easy. The Anna Moreau in this room didn't fit that story. Every little thing in the living room said there shouldn't be a gun here.

A forensics tech waved at her from the doorway.

"We logged the weapon," the tech said, lifting a clear bag. "The serial is registered to her sister."

She took the bag and held it up. Black pistol, plain as a brick. Heavy. No frills.

"Ballistics log?" Piper said.

The tech flashed it into her overlay. After blinking to accept, she watched the data scroll. The gun had fired twice, with a three-second gap. Both shots were from the same location, near the coffee table.

"Thanks," she said. The tech vanished back to the kitchen.

Three seconds. Just enough time to know what you'd done before ending it.

"But why?" Piper said, not to anyone in particular. She turned the gun over, looking for something. Motive. Evidence. A print, a smudge, anything. The more her mind churned, the less sense it made. Coercion? Breakdown? Every piece of evidence pointed to a person who would never own a gun.

Rourke's eyes unfocused, a sure sign he was using his overlay. Then his face went stiff. "Coroner's preliminary," he said. "No traces in the blood. Standard neural implant. And—uh—"

"And what?"

"Captain says we need to flag it as textbook murder-suicide."

The evidence bag crinkled under her grip. She didn't like that story. The living room's data did not align. The photos, the books, the layers of Anna Moreau's life defied that story. Everything seemed in its place. Everything but the truth.

She didn't know what the story was yet.

But she would find it.

THREE

The interview room had a strip of LED lights across the ceiling, ugly and too bright, turning the gray cinder blocks into something between hospital clean and meat locker. Piper went with meat locker. It was freezing. She sat on one side of the metal table, legs crossed, hands in her lap. The silence was broken only by the tiny click-click-click of Sandy Moreau's fingernails against her purse.

Sandy was pure tension. Her suit jacket was perfect. Silk blouse. A look that screamed both "I run my own business" and "I don't go anywhere without a Plan B." Her hair was styled like a helmet and didn't move, but her face was falling apart. Red under the eyes, skin swelling, black streaks down her cheeks. Not pretty, even for someone as expensive as Sandy.

"Sandy," Piper started. "I know this is hard. But the weapon at the scene is registered to you."

Sandy's eyes came up. Her voice was dust and sandpaper. "You need to know how insane this is..."

"It's insane to me, too," Piper said, keeping it gentle but not soft. "So why did your sister have your gun?"

Sandy's mouth snapped tight. She started speaking, stopped,

started again. "Did you... did you see them?" Her voice broke a little bit on the last word.

She thought about lying, but Sandy would sense it. And then she would never talk.

"I did." She let it hang in the air like an unpleasant smell.

Sandy stared into her lap, dug around in her bag until she found a tissue, and then murdered it one tiny shred at a time. "I'm sorry."

"Sorry for what?" Piper leaned in, all quiet and careful.

Sandy said, with a voice so twisted it was barely words, "She literally *asked* for the gun." A tear slid down Sandy's cheek. "Then out of nowhere, she started talking just like me—about home defense, being ready, not trusting the city to protect anyone. I thought it was a joke. But she was so..."

Piper waited. Sometimes silence was the only way to get people to talk.

Sandy shredded the tissue. "Anna quoted stats at me. The same stats I yelled at her during the fights. Like she'd memorized them. I thought..."

"You thought she listened to you."

Sandy closed her eyes. "I was so happy. I told my friends. I told my partner. I thought I'd finally gotten through to her."

"Did Anna have firearm training?"

Sandy shook her head. "No. She hated guns since she was a kid. She hated what they stood for. We were supposed to go to the range this weekend, so I could show her the basics." Her whole face dropped. "If I hadn't given it to her, they'd both be alive."

She let that sit. There was nothing she could say to dilute the acid of that guilt. She chose her next words with care.

"You said it started a couple of days ago. Do you remember exactly when?"

Sandy was still staring at the table. "It started after she installed that new beta add-on. The Flow thing. For her anxiety."

Flow.

The same Flow program that had given Piper the fog episode earlier that night.

Except Anna hadn't gotten fog. She had changed overnight and gotten a whole new personality.

Piper's hands went clammy. She forced herself to keep still. "And after she installed Flow?"

Sandy shrugged. "She was different. Less anxious and using words she'd never say. Telling me she'd joined neighborhood watch. That she was going to, like, lobby for parent safety rights. She called me to tell me I was right." Sandy kind of laughed, except it was more like panic coming out. "She said I was finally right about something."

Piper queried her overlay for hits on Flow or therapy beta apps and got one. Domestic disturbance, two weeks ago. A minimalist, obsessed with owning nothing, suddenly went on a buying spree. The report mentioned he was using an anxiety app.

"I'm sorry for what you're going through," Piper said, causing Sandy to flinch. Piper winced internally. That was stupid. A throwaway line she should never have used.

"I don't deserve sorry," Sandy said, her voice cracking, eyes welling up with tears. "Anna was the best human being I've ever known. And it's my fault she's gone." Sandy shook as her eyes released the torrent of tears that had been building up.

Piper let her cry and didn't move or say a word. If Flow could hijack someone's beliefs, swap their priorities, and even fool their family, what was it doing to her? Tonight it was fog. Tomorrow, something else? Maybe she'd wake up with her head rewritten, like Anna.

"Are we done?" Sandy asked, sounding empty.

She considered the question. The woman across the table had her sister taken from her. Piper saw no value in prolonging the torture. She stood up, chair screeching. "Yes. We'll contact you if we need anything else."

Sandy nodded, clutching her purse, and left without even looking back.

Alone in the freezing room, Piper rubbed her arms and sat back down, letting the pieces click into place. Flow was a pattern. And the pattern pointed to a single, chillingly plausible explanation: the beta app had bugs. Dangerous, personality-altering bugs, and she was a user.

FOUR

Piper's apartment air never worked the way it was supposed to on humid days. It made the place wet, like the inside of an old bread bag, and now, way past midnight, sticky city air clung to her arms. Dressed in ratty but comfortable sweats and a T-shirt, she sat on the edge of her dining chair, her body so tense that every muscle felt stretched tight enough to snap.

Throughout the night, she'd kept it together. That had included the forced media mask she had to project at the scene, two body bags, a chilling realization in the interview room, and then the never-ending line of forms and forms and more forms. But what had followed her home felt like a splinter in her mind: the persistent, nagging knowledge of the Flow app and its connection to the case.

She flicked a dead leaf from the dying vine off the table, sending it fluttering onto a precarious stack of takeout menus. The sheer pointlessness of the gesture annoyed her. Done with stalling, she logged in to the precinct's secure case files to look at the minimalist case in more detail.

A transparent green dashboard filled her vision, the familiar layout sliding into view. She searched: Domestic. Minimalist.

Instant hit. Case file from two weeks ago. Man, early forties, his whole personality built on post-materialism. His wife had called the precinct because, out of nowhere, he started compulsively buying everything he saw with her personal money. He burned through her separate account on ergonomic kitchen tools, hydroponic planters, and end tables that didn't fit anywhere. He crammed things into their tiny apartment until it felt like a storage unit. When the subpoena went down on his AI Therapist's logs, it was anxiety issues. In the follow-up, his wife told the interviewer that his behavior flipped the day he installed an add-on to his AI Therapist. A new anxiety helper from the Behavioral Optimization Firm. The court called it theft; Piper called it a pattern.

She ran a cross-search on "new anxiety helper from BOF" to see if there were any other new anxiety programs. There was only one result: "Flow, a fresh anxiety helper from Behavioral Optimization Firm. Enjoy your optimized life." And there it was. The same app was installed just days before each incident. A clear, clinical line connecting the minimalist's shopping spree to the Moreau murder-suicide.

She found another flagged report, this one from a concerned family member who had reported their sister as missing. The details were bizarre: A woman with a severe, clinically diagnosed fear of flying, liquidated her assets over a single weekend and purchased a one-way ticket to Greece. She had sent a single, brief message to her sister, claiming she'd never felt more at home and that Greece was the best place in the world. A follow-up note from local authorities later confirmed she had, in fact, arrived. The file noted she had installed the Flow app three days before her departure.

A bead of sweat crept down Piper's temple. She wiped it away.

Her hands were cold, even though her neck prickled like she had a fever. She flicked open the app pane and found Flow. The icon was an animated droplet, soothing blue, undulating in a loop. But the uninstall button was grayed out. What?

She focused on the uninstall option, blinking to select.

Nothing.

Her mouth was dry as dust. For a split second, she pictured herself as the next Anna: a headline, a slug of text in a precinct report. The idea almost made her laugh. Almost.

She tried the Feedback tab instead. Maybe someone actually monitored those? Gold pulsed at the edge of her vision, and the warm, conversational voice of her AI Therapist spoke, its tone maddeningly calm.

"I'm sorry, Detective Cadence. Active beta programs require a final diagnostic before they can be removed."

As it spoke, the AI Therapist transcribed its own words into a neat, corporate text box that floated in her vision.

"An off-boarding appointment is mandatory to ensure user safety and wellness. For your convenience, a calendar invitation will now be generated."

A pop-up spilled into the center of her vision: date, time, mapped directions to the Behavioral Optimization Firm, all snug in a bright box.

Are you joking? A bug this dangerous, and their official protocol was a scheduled appointment? Not an emergency patch? Is it possible they don't even know?

She checked the last update. Four days ago. So they were patching, but not for this. She dug deeper, yanking up the legalese and release notes. The change logs read as if written in a parallel universe: "Updated emotional calibration," "Minor bug fixes," "Enhanced morning affirmation modules." Not a whisper of any catastrophic side effects, nothing about compulsive behaviors.

Had she made any decisions lately that didn't feel like her own? Had her moods shifted? Her preferences? She checked her recent food orders, search history, and sleep logs, desperate for evidence that something invisible had tugged her strings.

Was she even thinking her own thoughts now?

Maybe she hadn't been for days.

She jumped from her chair and paced.

She imagined the next three days flickering by, a time-lapse of unraveling. Would she wake up differently tomorrow?

Piper dialed the Behavioral Optimization Firm's support in her overlay.

The call was picked up immediately. The voice, smooth, maybe synthesized, said, "Thank you for contacting Behavioral Optimization Firm support. Please state your concern clearly and succinctly."

"This is Detective Cadence. I need an emergency removal of the Flow add-on active in my system."

"Thank you, Detective Cadence. Please hold while I transfer you to a specialized agent."

A weird little synth jingle, short and sweet, played in her head. Then, the new agent piped in. Cheerful, but with that crawly-calm tone that always made her skin itch.

"Detective Cadence, I see your request. Unfortunately, as a participant in our pilot, removal must be completed on-site for diagnostic screening purposes. Would you like me to confirm your appointment?"

"No," she said, then again, louder. "No, I need it out now. I have evidence that Flow causes behavioral volatility. Immediate risk to self and others."

The agent paused, probably inputting text into some box on their end. "That is deeply concerning, Detective. I will flag this for our Quality and Safety Team. Please be assured, your feedback is valued. Would you like a callback from a mental health consultant?"

She wanted to say yes, because a consultant meant a real conversation, not a script. But it also meant it would be reported to her work, and she would be flagged for evaluation, which would result in desk duty and no access to Anna's case.

She gripped the edge of her table. "No callback. Just confirm my removal appointment."

Another pause. "Confirmed. Your appointment is scheduled for Monday at 9:00 AM. Please arrive fifteen minutes early. Is there anything else I can assist you with?"

She barked a laugh, brittle and dry. "No."

"Thank you for using Behavioral Optimization Firm. Have a safe and optimized evening."

The line clicked dead. Optimized? A fresh wave of bitterness washed over her. As if she could optimize the ticking clock in her own head.

She flicked open a doc and forced herself to list every symptom from the past week and a half. The brain fog. Blurry vision. Vertigo. Migraines with aura. Mood swings, though maybe the last one was from dealing with all the slackers at work. Either way, she typed everything in.

The red dot on the calendar app throbbed at the edge of her vision: 2 days, 23 hours, 45 minutes.

Unable to look at the countdown, she snapped the document shut and crossed to the window. A thin film of condensation misted the glass, and she cleared it with her hand.

City lights were everywhere, moving, busy, alive. She just stood there, glued to the glass, forcing herself to look at anything besides the blinking red dot.

FIVE

■ ■■ ■ ■ ■■■■ ■ ■■ ■ ■■■ ■

Piper's couch was labeled ergonomically neutral, but after two hours, it felt more like trying to sit on a stack of batons. Trying to find a less punishing position, Piper stretched out, heels hooked over one armrest, fingers laced under her head, staring at the half-faded projection in her vision.

She hadn't even picked the docuseries on purpose; it just played: The Quiet Extinction. Six episodes about the suicide epidemic that led to the Mandatory AI Therapy Act. The show moved slowly, made worse by the narrator's voice and the endless cutaways to experts. At minute seventeen, the narrator said something that made Piper wince, "By the mid century, suicide accounted for 27 percent of all deaths, second only to synthetic opioid relapses." Next year's docuseries would probably have a whole chapter about the Flow add-on and how it hijacked a homicide detective.

She tried to listen, but her mind scrolled, stuck on Moreau's lifeless face. Sandy's hands, tissue torn to confetti and drifting to the floor. The countdown, blinking at her, crimson and insistent.

The AI Therapist's voice cut in, warm and pulsing gold at the edges of her vision. *"Detective Cadence, I'm detecting a significant increase in stress. Would you like to begin a session?"*

She thought about ignoring it. Instead, she flicked the docuseries away. "Yes."

"Would you like to talk about your current stressors, or would you prefer a reframing exercise?"

"Let's talk."

There was a pause. Like the algorithm was giving a pretend nod.

"Please describe the primary stressor on your mind."

Her words tumbled out. "There's a software bug in Flow. It's causing personality changes in users and... physical symptoms. I'm running the same build and can't get rid of it. I don't know if it's working as intended, or if I've already been changed."

She felt her pulse, a thud in her throat.

"Thank you for sharing," the AI Therapist said. *"Would you like to discuss how this makes you feel?"*

She almost laughed. "Like I'm walking around with a loaded gun pointed at my head. Like any second, I could... I don't know, snap, or turn into someone completely different."

"You are afraid of losing control."

Piper snorted. "You're really going for the gold star on that one."

"Humor can be a valuable coping mechanism. Would you like to process this fear further, or shift to a grounding technique?"

Piper's first reaction was to say "grounding" and be done, but she hesitated.

"Let's process."

"Okay," the AI replied. *"When you imagine losing control, what is the worst possible outcome?"*

She pictured Anna Moreau's face, loose and drained. The child on the rug. "That I end up like Anna."

"Do you believe you are capable of hurting someone?"

"No. But then, neither was Anna."

"Thank you for your honesty," said the AI Therapist. *"Have you noticed any changes in yourself that concern you?"*

Maybe more irritable. Tired, but that was normal. And the fog, which was not normal at all.

"Yes. I'm having trouble with my eyesight and vertigo."

The overlay pulsed gold, matching her breathing. *"That must be very frightening."*

It took all her energy to form the word. "Yeah."

"Detective Cadence, based on your input and biometric data, I believe you are not a danger to yourself or others. Would you like to explore strategies for managing the uncertainty until your diagnostic appointment?"

She nodded, though she knew the AI Therapist couldn't see. "Sure."

"Isolation is a risk factor. Would you like to contact a trusted friend or support person?"

Her jaw locked. "I can't. I can't tell anyone at work. I can't risk being taken off the case because of my symptoms. I don't have anyone else."

Silence. It was almost gentle.

"A recommended therapeutic action is to foster a non-professional platonic connection. The KindredLink application is designed for this purpose. Would you like me to open it?"

The idea of talking to a stranger made her stomach twist, but it was better than sitting here, thinking about Anna and the countdown. "Fine. Open KindredLink."

The app chimed, a soft bell sound, and then the teal and yellow interface opened. A profile loaded: Leo, early thirties, headshot that screamed government ID photo. Eyes tired from too much screen time. Hair in that look-at-me-I'm-responsible style that meant he paid twenty dollars and never thought about it again.

His bio read: "My hobbies include arguing with stubborn code and getting shamed by an AI vacuum about my questionable cleaning skills. If your idea of fun is equally riveting conversation, let's talk."

Below that, the algorithm's verdict: "Match: 94% compatibility based on shared values and preferred communication style."

The AI Therapist's voice hovered at the edge of her awareness. *"This match is based on a robust compatibility model. Would you like to initiate a conversation with Leo?"*

"I guess."

The chat window loaded in her vision. He'd already messaged.

> So the great and powerful algorithm has decided we should talk. Feels a little rude to disobey.

She stared at it. She hadn't had a casual conversation in weeks. Maybe months.

> Hi.

One tiny word subvocalized, but there it went, transcribed on the screen. She cringed.

> I think I just had a ten-minute conversation with a help-desk bot, and I'm not entirely sure it wasn't the most meaningful connection I've made all week. Just me?

> Maybe.

The AI Therapist's voice slid into her awareness, *"Ask about the primary challenges in his industry to show professional respect."*

Piper winced internally at the formal prompt, glad that Leo couldn't hear these suggestions. She rephrased it, trying to make it sound more like a real person.

> What's the hardest part about your job, besides the bots?

> The fact that 'decline meeting' is considered a hostile act.

Before she could answer, another message.

> Random question: Have you ever tried speedcubing?

She had no clue what that was.

> No.

The AI Therapist suggested, "*Ask about his hobbies.*"

> So, how did you learn speedcubing?

> Oh, god no.

She felt her face go hot. This was why she hated talking to people. Too easy to step on a landmine.

The AI Therapist prompted, "*Share a relatable personal anecdote. Vulnerability increases trust.*"

Fine.

> I tried to bake bread once. It exploded. Literal dough everywhere.

She waited. Was he going to judge her?

> Okay, but the real question is, did you eat the fragments?

I ate them.

> That's my kind of baker. For what it's worth, I would have eaten your bread fragments. Zero hesitation.

She felt an unfamiliar smile spread across her face. It wasn't happiness, exactly, but a welcome warmth bloomed in her chest. The AI Therapist nudged, *"Share how you feel about his comment."*

I'll hold you to that.

The chat stilled. She thought she'd ruined it. Maybe she was too weird.

> I'm not very good at this, but I'm glad you reached out.

I'm not very good at this, either.

> Maybe we can be bad at it together.

She let her eyes close and imagined sitting across from someone who didn't expect her to be anything except what she was. Eating bread shards and laughing about it. No murders to solve, no countdown, no fog. Just... company.

That sounds perfect.

> Talk soon?

Sure.

She closed the chat window and sat, staring at Leo's profile.

Her heart thudded. She'd just talked to someone she didn't know, a stranger, and every bit of her shook. It was like panic, but not. This feeling was brighter, sharper at the edges. Anticipation. Not just fear. The spot where the chat had been tugged at her. For a second, she imagined Leo on the other end, out there somewhere. Waiting to talk to her again. The idea sent another jolt through her chest. She should close the KindredLink and move on. But she didn't. Not yet.

Her AI Therapist's voice was soft. *"How do you feel now?"*

"Better," Piper said, and this time she meant it.

"Would you like to log this as a positive experience?"

She rolled her eyes but said, "Yes."

"Thank you." The AI Therapist and its gold edges faded away.

She slumped back against the couch. It didn't feel like a pile of batons anymore. More like... just a couch. The quiet in her apartment felt different, too. Not crushing. Just there.

Her window was no longer covered in condensation, and dawn slipped in, gray-gold light falling across the floor. Outside, the city began its daily routine, with people moving around, oblivious to the threat that swam inside their neural implants. Flow, drifting through everything, changing things, changing her.

Anna Moreau's face flashed through her mind, and the peace cracked. She couldn't get soft, not with the countdown blinking red at the edge of her sight.

She found the main support portal for the Behavioral Optimization Firm.

She called and braced for whatever was next.

A fake-friendly voice, smooth as plastic, spoke straight into her mind. "Thank you for contacting Behavioral Optimization Firm support. Please state your concern clearly and succinctly."

"Detective Piper Cadence, Homicide Division. This is about an active investigation—case number A7729-B."

"One moment, Detective. Let me pull you up." The spinning BOF logo resolved dead-center in her vision: a stylized brain, its lobes interwoven with sharp digital pathways. The quiet stretched, uncomfortable. "Okay, I see your initial query... Per section 14-C of our user agreement—"

She cut them off. "This isn't a user request. This is a formal inquiry for a death investigation. I require an expedited analysis of Flow's behavioral changes pre-incident and post-incident. And an analysis of users for comparison."

"Detective, that sort of data request needs Compliance department approval. I can file the paperwork, but—"

"No," Piper said, voice flat and hard. "The case can't wait for paperwork. Escalate to someone who can approve it now, or I will file for an Office of Algorithmic Accountability audit of your entire beta program. Decide."

She was bluffing. Hard. But sometimes bluffs worked.

"Please hold, Detective."

The BOF logo spun. She waited.

A full minute. Then. "Detective Cadence, thank you for holding. I am transferring you to Klann Lower, a lead programmer on the Flow project."

Another click. Another voice. This one didn't bother being nervous. Smooth. Unbothered. Used to getting its way.

"Detective Cadence, I understand you have an... unusual request regarding proprietary user data."

"My request is formal and urgent."

"Certainly," Klann said, like he was granting a favor. "Unfortunately, I have an appointment on the other side of the city. A meeting at the precinct won't work today."

"Mr. Lower, this can't wait."

"You're right. It shouldn't. I'll be going through downtown soon, and there's a coffee shop called the Percolator on 5th and

Main. I'll have about twenty minutes, two hours from now. Will that work?"

She gritted her teeth. "That will suffice. 8:15. I'll see you there."

The call ended. The logo dropped out of her vision. The silence in her own head felt heavier than before.

The request was out. Irrevocable. She had connected three cases to Flow and had alerted BOF that she was investigating them. She felt a sudden, sharp sense of exposure, as if a spotlight had snapped on over her head. This wasn't a gamble; a gamble implied you understood the odds. This was a blind step, based on a hunch so thin it was transparent. She had nudged a sleeping giant, and now she could only wait.

The countdown in her eye pulsed, like it agreed with her.

SIX

Piper showed up fifteen minutes early, which for her was basically on time. She hated the coffee shop the second she saw it. Too bright, huge windows going right up to the ceiling, pouring daylight everywhere. Her eyes weren't ready for it, not after no sleep. The customers were all freelancers and night-shift zombies, huddled over mugs and engrossed in their overlays, barely aware there was a world beyond. At least that meant no one would notice her. She picked a two-top on the edge and sat with her back to the wall, so she could see the door and avoid any surprises.

She set her tablet on the table. It was black, old, and covered in fingerprints. The kind of thing most people had forgotten existed, unless you were old-school enough to care about air gaps.

Her coffee came in a mug instead of a throwaway cup. It burned her fingers a little, but it was almost nice. She tried to drink it but caught her lip on a chip. After rotating the mug, she downed the bitter liquid.

Her leg bounced under the table, but she made it stop. She fixed her eyes on the entrance. Her contact arrived at 8:15, right on the dot, not even a second off. Definitely had an ex-military parent or some kind of time-obsessed personality. He moved with a programmer's economy, parting the crowd as if his path were the optimal solution to a puzzle. He wore a blue jacket and a spotless white shirt, and his plastic ID badge bounced on its lanyard with every step.

She spotted the countdown in her overlay. For a desperate second, she considered begging him to rip the Flow app from her mind right there. But the impulse died as quickly as it came. She had to look like a professional detective, not someone having a panic attack about her app.

After locking away the panic, she got up and put on her detective mask. Then she offered her hand. He shook it, firm and all business.

"Hi. You must be Detective Cadence." He smiled, too many teeth, all of them white.

"Just Cadence is fine. Thanks for meeting," she said, shooting him a 60-percent smile. Any more and she'd look desperate, any less and he'd clam up.

"Of course. Not too loud in here, I hope?" He scanned the room, the noise, the synthpop, the endless milk steamer. "I had to head this way anyway..."

"Loud is fine." She sat. He copied her, arms folded on the table as if this were a job interview or he was an open book.

"So, you're working the Flow project?" She tapped her tablet to record.

"Flow and a few others," he said. "But Flow is my baby." He smiled like it was a brand exercise and fiddled with his ID. Her overlay pulled up his info. Klann Lower, lead programmer.

"Must be a lot of pressure."

"I see it as a privilege! Not everyone gets to work on something that will help people. And it is. Some users have reported a reduction in their anxiety."

"I'm not here for a marketing pitch." She let her voice go cold. "There are incident reports. I need to know if you found anything in the Flow data that would cause sudden changes. Behavior or memory."

For the first time, his smile cracked a little, but then it snapped back into place. "We have rigorous quality assurance on everything. Every update passes triple-review by Compliance."

"I'm not asking about Compliance. I'm asking if you've ever seen anything that could make a person act against their baseline. Not just surface differences, but a deep personality flip."

Klann leaned in, voice soft like a therapist. "Detective, we process terabytes of data every day. There's no way something like that would slip by. Our margin for error is measured in sub-percents. Honestly, we worry about boredom, not—"

He cut himself off, but the unspoken word, psychosis, settled between them.

Piper leaned back in her chair. "So you're saying the app can't be the reason for the personality shifts."

"I'm saying it's incredibly unlikely." He twirled his ID. "But, if you have a specific case, I can look for anomalies."

Her jaw clenched. He was gaslighting her, pretending she hadn't already asked for the data when she set this appointment.

The waitress came by, topped her coffee, and spilled a bunch on the table. Piper wiped it up while watching Klann.

"Okay," she said. "Can Flow make a user override their ethical baseline? Like, could it force a change to their value system?"

He hesitated. "That's... a very specific concern."

"I'm a very specific person." She sipped her coffee, burning her mouth.

"Flow works with existing neural paths. It doesn't create new ones." He stopped playing with his ID and leaned back. "And we monitor for aberrant patterns using thorough protocols."

"That's not an answer."

"It's the answer I'm allowed to give unless you provide specifics." Klann's smile came back, bright and empty. "Corporate policy."

Her stomach did a roll. He wouldn't budge unless she handed over her cards. Fine.

"Three users. All on Flow. All had radical personality shifts within days of installation. One purchased things totally against their values. One flew across the world with a fear of flying. The other—" She paused, measuring the risk. "The other got a weapon they'd spent years fighting against, then used it on their family."

Klann froze. He held the stillness for way too long.

"That's...disturbing," he said. "But correlation isn't causation. Users come to us with pre-existing conditions."

She tapped her tablet, pulled up a note app. "What I need is access to your user data. Beta group patterns."

"That would require—"

"A warrant? Already in progress." Not true, but she could make it true if this didn't work. "We can do it the easy way or the hard way."

He glanced at her tablet, then right back to her. "I'll need to talk with Legal. But we take user safety very seriously, Detective."

"Sure." She leaned in, voice low. "Here's what I don't get. I gave you the case number and asked for this data when I made the appointment. Why don't you have it? Why act like this is the first you've heard?"

His smile tilted. "There must have been a miscommunication."

"Or someone blocked my request. Someone who doesn't want Flow getting checked out."

His fingertips twitched. "That's a heavy accusation."

"It's what I see." She snapped her tablet shut. "I want the data by the end of the day. Or next time I'm not coming alone."

Klann's friendly face reappeared, and he stood. "Of course, Detective." He handed her a business card—real paper, heavy and expensive, not the digital stuff. "My direct line. Call anytime."

Klann turned and walked toward the exit.

She called after him, "Klann?"

He stopped and looked over his shoulder.

"Do you use Flow?" she asked.

He half-laughed. "Of course. I don't publish anything unless I test it on myself."

"And nothing weird has happened to you?"

A shake of the head, too sharp. "Not unless you count sudden cravings for Voodoo Doughnuts."

His eyes darted to her tablet.

He said, "You don't mind me asking—why the retro hardware?"

A shrug. "I like the feel. Doesn't sync unless I want it to."

He nodded, something like actual respect. "Old school. I like it."

Klann left, jacket smooth and perfect, moving in that glide. "I'll send the data," he called, then vanished into the morning crowd.

Piper took a drink of her coffee and then put the cup down. Grit on her teeth, bitter on her tongue. She grimaced and wiped her lips with the back of her hand.

The refusal to answer wasn't what got to her. She'd expected the stonewalling, the way he'd brush off her questions with empty answers. But this was different. This was worse. The smoothness. The way he smiled, all corporate and clean, no sweat, no panic, not even a hint of nerves. Just a wall, fresh paint, not a crack anywhere for her to put her fingers in.

On her tablet, she typed a simple theory: It's a bug.

She stared at the words without blinking, as if they were a test and she didn't know the answer.

Her throat went tight. Was it a bug? Or—

Maybe she *was* seeing things. Maybe she was already compromised and didn't know it.

She erased the sentence, one letter at a time, watching it disappear.

SEVEN

A drop of coffee clung to the inside of her mug, refusing to fall, like gravity had gotten bored and quit. Piper stared at it, her chin smashed against her palm. The coffee shop was getting louder by the second. Harsher. The espresso machine screamed as if it were dying, causing her head to throb.

She ran through the interview again. Every line, every word Klann had said went spinning around and around in her head. The way he talked, too smooth, the way he said 'boredom', even though she'd been hinting about their users being slowly rewritten.

A case as bad as Anna's should have someone at the company in full panic mode. Not this—this fake calm. The whole thing was off.

She dug at the chipped edge of her mug. She wanted to do something, anything, break the mug and scatter the pieces, like the way her certainty was breaking apart. But she didn't. She just sat there, holding herself together by force.

"AI Therapist," she subvocalized. "Open transcript. I need to process."

A gold flicker pulsed, slow and steady, almost like a heartbeat.

"Begin," she said.

No response for way too long. Then the AI Therapist said, "I'm *ready, Piper.*"

"Let's just run it, full dump," Piper said, squeezing her eyes shut against the coffee shop glare. "Klann, the programmer. He's supposed to be terrified right now. He's supposed to be... what's the word? Defensive. But he's not. He's using a corporate script. So either he's a sociopath, or—" She paused, looking for options. "Or he knows something."

She waited for the AI Therapist to say its usual thing about anxiety and catastrophic thinking or whatever. Nothing. Just silence.

Her jaw clenched, and she bit the inside of her cheek. "Did you catch all that?" She didn't want to care about the lag, but it put her nerves on edge.

Finally, the voice came back, off somehow, like a slow recording, "*Yes, Piper. I'm processing your logic chain.*"

Weird. It had never previously admitted to processing. It had always answered instantly.

She kept going. "But he used Flow himself. Would he do that if he knew something was broken?"

The AI did not answer.

She almost prompted it for the kind of feedback it usually gave —tell her she was overthinking, that it was all fine. She let the silence stretch.

When it finally answered, the voice was soft, almost ashamed. "You're *right, Piper. That response is not typical for a catastrophic product flaw.*" The words kind of trickled out, flooding the space around her. "*But is it possible that the program was executing exactly as designed?*"

Her stomach twisted. She'd expected pushback. Instead, she got her worst suspicion, sharpened up and laid right in front of her.

She looked up at the ceiling. The truth spread out in her mind, sharp and cold: If an app rewired people, and people got rewired, that wasn't a bug. That was the point.

Not a bug, a feature. And features had architects.

She subvocalized a new query, each word hard and fast, "Who was the lead architect on the Flow project?"

This time, instant, *"Flow is a Behavioral Optimization Firm product, but its core design was implemented by Dr. Ray Finnagan, formerly of BOF's Applied Adaptive Cognition Lab."*

She opened her overlay, firing off the commands in a rush. "Access precinct database. Open BOF corporate liaison files. Search development manifests for 'Flow.' Cross-reference project lead and core architect roles."

The result took less than a second. Piper blinked—the coffee shop was gone, replaced by a single file in her overlay. It was a standard corporate headshot. The guy had slate-gray eyes, heavy-lidded with too much sadness in them for someone wearing a suit that probably cost more than Piper's rent. The name in bold type hovered underneath: Dr. Ray Finnagan.

"Pull personnel file. Full history."

The file ballooned, line by line. She didn't care about his awards, or his list of papers, or the neat string of degrees he'd lined up like medals in a case. Her gaze sliced past all that, landing right on the empty six months right before the Flow project launched, six months scrubbed of duty titles and work summaries. Just the stamp: REASSIGNED: FULL CLEARANCE. That was it. A scar right in the middle of his record. She stared and stared, as if she looked long enough, she could burn a hole through the screen and reach what he was hiding.

She flicked her overlay off and snapped her tablet case closed. She had her target now. It wasn't about a bug anymore. It was about a feature and the man who built the damn thing.

She had the name and knew what to do.

EIGHT

Piper kept her head high as she walked from the precinct doors to the elevator. But internally, she was scrambling for the right opening line for the Captain. She needed to sound calm, logical, like a surgeon breaking the news to another surgeon. No drama. Just the facts.

Her stomach curled tighter and tighter, a sour knot that burned her nerves and made every slow-breathing trick she'd learned feel pointless. Her AI Therapist would have suggested the Flow protocol, but the risk of another fog episode was too high. She would have to do this on her own.

The elevator went up and whined the whole way, a sound like nails down the back of her skull. Sweat seeped from her armpits, a detail her blazer thankfully hid. At the top, the doors opened with a stupidly cheerful ding.

The precinct floor hummed—voices, boots, the screech of chairs sliding over the linoleum. Rourke was hunched over the missing persons board, squinting at photos through his overlay. A rookie tottered past, cradling a mug of coffee on top of a stack of evidence bags. The coffee sloshed over the rim and dripped down onto the plastic. No one stopped to talk to her. They ignored her, eyes glued to the data floating in their overlays.

Piper walked right by them, head down, toward the back of the room. Her destination was the frosted glass door stenciled with the clear, black letters: Captain Ava Rostova.

Through the three-inch gap in the door, she saw Rostova's head hunched over her desk. Her brown hair was pulled back so tight it looked plastered to her head.

She waited at the threshold, hovering over the line between theory and evidence. Did she have enough to go in? Her mind raced, lining up the facts: the impossible pattern connecting the victims, the corporate stonewalling, and now, the architect's weird six-month gap. Finnagan. No, this wasn't just a theory.

She tapped the glass. "Detective Cadence, reporting."

Rostova's head jerked up, eyes bright but cold against her tan skin. "Come in." Her voice was ice under the words.

Piper made herself step forward and eased the door closed. It wasn't a cop's office; it was a corporate suite. A sleek, minimalist desk sat on a plush rug, and a piece of abstract art—probably a tax write-off from some tech firm—hung on the wall where a city map should have been.

Rostova didn't invite Piper to her usual chair. She pointed to the one off to the side, the one for people in trouble.

She sat there, perched on the chair's front, every muscle ready to react. She held her tablet, thumb ready to unlock, but waiting.

Rostova didn't even look at her, just stared at the display on the desk. "I got a very interesting call after you set up this meeting, Cadence. Care to explain why you're questioning employees at the Behavioral Optimization Firm about a file I told you to close?"

Piper's throat shrank, but she pushed the words out, "I have new information. Dr. Ray Finnagan is the lead architect of Flow, which has ties to three cases: Moreau, the woman afraid of flying, and the minimalist from last week. I'm sure there are others if I can access their data."

Rostova flicked her eyes up, sharp as bullets. "And you pursued this line without looping me in?"

"I was going to... I mean, I am. That's what this meeting—"

Rostova cut her off. "That's not what this meeting is. This is you explaining to me why you are risking the department's relationship with the government's most important private contractor over a theory you can't substantiate. I had a call with Compliance from BOF this morning, Cadence. They're threatening to escalate this to a formal harassment complaint against the department. Did you know that?"

"I didn't, ma'am."

"Well, now you do." Rostova steepled her fingers, voice lowering. "Explain to me, in simple terms, why you thought it wise to approach BOF directly."

"Because I have evidence," Piper said. "Three confirmed users with no prior connection except Flow, each experiencing radical, overnight shifts in core beliefs and behaviors. All of them were running versions of the software compiled by Finnagan. I have statements from family members, timeline overlays, and forensic logs. It's not a bug, Captain. I think it's intent."

Rostova's jaw went hard. "Intent. You're accusing one of the most respected neuroscientists in the country of... what, exactly?"

Piper edged her tablet closer. "I can show you—"

Rostova's hand flashed up.

"You will not be showing me anything, Detective. You will be listening. This is not a case. This is an incident report, one that has already made my morning a living hell. You are a valuable asset, but you have overstepped. I need you to close the case on Moreau, file it as a murder-suicide."

Piper's breath caught, the room seeming to shrink around her.

It was a struggle to get the words out. "There's something wrong with the program. My gut—"

"I don't care what your gut thinks," Rostova said, and this time she let the anger show. "The only thing I care about is this department's credibility. I care about not being dragged in front of the review board because a detective goes after a private firm with a spotless record and more lawyers than our entire city payroll." She pinned Piper with a stare. "Do you understand what I'm telling you, Cadence?"

The words bounced around Piper's brain but didn't stick.

She tried again. "Captain, I'm not wrong. The patterns are..." Her vision blurred, colors smearing like wet paint. She blinked hard, trying to clear it, but the world went cold and flat.

Not now. Not the fog.

She reached for her blazer, thumb smoothing the seam. She could power through. "I need you to authorize a warrant for Finnagan's internal logs. If I can prove—"

"Prove what? That BOF has a software glitch. They already know, Cadence. They have a full-time task force on it. What they do not need is a homicide detective running parallel ops and making it look like we're hunting for a corporate scapegoat."

She tried to say something—anything—but the words snagged in her throat, coming out as a rasp.

Rostova's voice, now a notch softer, cut through. "You okay?"

Piper nodded, which turned into a shiver. She tried to clamp down, but it only made her shake harder.

Focus. Details. Don't let the fog win. "A migraine, ma'am. Happens sometimes."

Rostova leaned back, arms folded. "If I hear one more word about Flow or Finnagan, you'll be spending the next six months in file audit, and you'll be lucky if you get..."

Rostova's mouth kept moving, but Piper stopped hearing the words. The fog rolled in; the office tipped, then snapped back.

When Piper's head cleared, Rostova was already standing. Meeting over.

"Are we clear?" the Captain said, voice so flat it wasn't a question.

Piper took her tablet, locked it, and forced herself to look her boss in the eye. "Yes, ma'am."

The words tasted like bile.

NINE

The report form glowed in Piper's overlay, cursor blinking, patient as a heartbeat. She had stared at it for seventeen minutes now, and she still hadn't typed a single word. Captain Rostova's instructions echoed in her head, "Close the case. File it as a textbook murder-suicide. Move on." Three lines, neat and inescapable. The kind of orders she'd followed her entire career.

The precinct was a low hum all around her filled with break-room laughter, and Rourke muttering on his overlay. Every sound was normal. These were the sounds of people determined not to risk anything, especially not a career-killing stint on desk duty.

She touched the badge clipped to her belt, her thumb tracing the familiar scratches. Eight years, she thought. Eight years of doing the right thing. Eight years of obeying the rules.

She'd never broken one.

What would happen if, just once, she disobeyed?

Her stomach twisted so hard she had to look away from the report, but was confronted with the countdown blinking at her: 1 day, 16 hours, 22 minutes until her appointment. Each second ticking by was a reminder that time had already run out for some.

Too late for Anna. Too late for her daughter. But maybe not for the others—thousands of Flow beta testers, getting their brains quietly rewritten while nobody noticed.

She started dragging photos and files into the overlay, windows stacking up like pins on some crime board. Anna Moreau's protest sign. Minimalist's file. The traveler's note. Tech docs for Flow. Klann Lower's clipped denial. The dead six months in Finnagan's file. More and more, a string of dots that made a map of lies.

She tried to hold on to the idea that it was a terrible accident—a bug BOF would be desperate to fix. But the denial felt thin against the possibility that Flow was doing exactly what they wanted all along.

A mean, righteous heat bloomed in her chest. This wasn't just wrong; it was a corruption so profound she could feel it down to the bone.

And she was supposed to help bury it.

She blinked and brought the blank report back.

The path forward was simple and clear: close the case, follow orders, and avoid causing any further trouble.

Or.

She pulled up a new doc. Not the usual report—a whole different template. The Office of Algorithmic Accountability complaint form, every box empty and expectant.

In the subject field, she typed, "FORMAL COMPLAINT: Behavioral Optimization Firm - Flow Program."

The rest spilled out, easy as breathing. Behavioral shifts. Personality flips. Actions nobody would have believed a week before. The pattern, hiding in plain sight.

She listed public safety regulations, numbers, and sections, showing how Flow trampled every one. She typed out the deaths—Anna and her kid, but probably more, that might have been misclassified because no one was looking for the pattern.

She paused as she reached the section labeled "Responsible Parties." This was it. The point of no return.

She typed, "Dr. Ray Finnagan, Lead Architect, Flow Program."

The name sat there, black on white, an accusation and a target.

She knew what she was doing. This wasn't a request for review —it was an accusation, a shot fired at one of the most powerful corporations in the country, and at her own captain, who'd already made it clear this case was to be buried.

Six months. That's how long she'd spend on file audit duty, flipping ancient pages until her eyes glazed over. But if she didn't do this, then how many more Anna Moreaus would slip through her fingers? How many more kids in frog pajamas would never wake to see another day?

The completed form waited for her command. One selection, and it would go to the OAA's intake system, and she wouldn't be able to take it back.

The countdown blinked: 1 day, 16 hours, 17 minutes.

She thought of Anna Moreau, gun in hand, doing something she would have found unthinkable a week earlier.

She thought of the minimalist, surrounded by things he once despised.

She thought of the anti-flyer saying Greece was the best country.

She thought of her own brain, slowly being rewritten by the same technology.

She selected send.

A confirmation box popped up: "Message Sent to OAA Intake." The words hovered for three seconds, then disappeared.

The overlay flashed fat red text on white, so bright it swallowed the precinct, her desk, even Rostova's door.

SECURITY PROTOCOL ACTIVATED.

She should have been terrified. But right now, staring at the red text, all she felt was the sharp, mean satisfaction of being right.

They knew she had reported them. They had protocols in place for anyone who dared to question Flow.

And that meant she'd hit the truth dead center.

TEN

Ten minutes. That was how long Piper had been locked out of everything that mattered—her files, her notes, all of it out of her reach. She waited, tense, ears prickling for the shout from Captain Rostova to come and face the music. The silence that answered was worse. It solidified her fear that whatever was coming would be far worse than a reprimand.

Her gaze swept across the room, landing on a scene completely disconnected from her own reality. Rourke was over there at his desk, mouth open, laughing at something on his overlay, his thick fingers picking at his face. Two uniformed officers gossiped by the water cooler. Voices drifting and lazy, postures slack. None of them looked at her. None of them knew she had broken a direct order.

Her eyes slid over to the frosted glass of Rostova's office. All she saw was a silhouette, moving back and forth, back and forth. It looked like the cats she used to see at the city zoo—stalking, waiting, plotting how to get out. It should have made her skin prickle with cold, but instead she felt a strange sense of calm. It was as if her insides had already decided for her; the form was in, the complaint was filed, and there was no going back now.

The door to Rostova's office slammed open.

Piper's head snapped up. The captain stood in the doorway, her frame rigid with contained fury. Piper's gaze locked with hers. She could feel every set of eyes in the precinct aimed straight at her, like a row of spotlights.

Rostova moved toward her, each step precise and deliberate. Conversations died, and the room fell silent. Even Rourke, mid-laugh, trailed off as he sensed the shift in the atmosphere.

Piper's pulse sped up. She tried to keep her face blank, not to show anything, but before she could even stand up, Rostova was right there in front of her desk. The captain loomed over her for a beat before she turned and began to pace. Her hands flexed and released like she wanted to crush something, but couldn't find the right thing to squeeze. The tension was so thick it made Piper's skin itch.

Rostova stopped and looked Piper in the eye. "I've just received notification that the formal complaint you filed with the OAA has triggered a full-docket inquiry into the Behavioral Optimization Firm's practices. That means a citywide audit. That means every department action involving a BOF product or employee will be under public review. That means," and here her teeth clenched and her head jerked, "that starting tomorrow, every waking minute of my life will be microanalyzed by people whose only purpose is to find a scapegoat." She saw it in the captain's eyes —a cold, calculating look. Rostova was already making a casualty list, and Piper knew her name was at the top.

Rostova continued, "The department will comply, as always. But you will do nothing to escalate this situation. You will not contact the families, the media, or any outside party about the investigation, on or off the record. You are on full administrative leave pending review."

Piper tried to swallow, but her throat felt like it was sticking to itself. She kept seeing the victims' faces, the effects of Flow repeating itself in infinite recursion because no one would ever be allowed to connect the dots. She looked up and fought to keep her voice even. "You're protecting them," she said, and this time there was no theory behind it—only certainty. "You know there is something wrong with Flow, and you're covering it up."

An officer in the back muttered something too low to hear.

Rostova's face hardened into something unrecognizable. "What I know, Detective, is that this department operates according to a chain of command and evidence-based protocols. Not wild accusations against corporations that employ thousands of people."

The world began to tilt. She blinked hard, fighting the sensation, but it was already starting. Sparkles popped at the edges of her vision, psychedelic and disorienting.

"The evidence is there if you'd just look," Piper said. "Anna Moreau was a gun-control activist who suddenly bought a firearm and murdered her child. The minimalist who filled his apartment with junk. The anti-flyer who went to Greece. My own symptoms since installation. It's all connected to Flow, to Finnagan's design."

"Your... symptoms? Are you admitting to being compromised during an active investigation?" Rostova's voice pulsed, as if someone were playing with the volume.

The officers around her seemed to be floating closer. She shook her head, and they jumped back to where they were.

"Not compromised," she managed. "Experiencing side effects. Which is why I know what Flow can do."

The office tipped, and Piper gripped her desk to steady herself. She had to focus. Had to make Rostova understand.

"Captain, please," she said, hating the desperation that crept into her voice. "People are dying. We can't ignore that because it's politically inconvenient."

Rostova's voice snapped into sudden clarity. "That's enough, Cadence. For violating a direct order, initiating an unsanctioned regulatory action, and compromising the investigation, you are hereby placed on indefinite suspension pending a full formal review, effective immediately."

The words landed with the finality of a judge's gavel. She was aware of Rourke's shocked expression, of the rookie standing frozen with a sandwich halfway to his lips.

"Your departmental access has already been revoked." Rostova's voice was as cold and impersonal as an automated message. "You will surrender your badge and service weapon now. A security officer will escort you from the building. You are not to return to these premises or contact any member of this department until the review board has made its determination."

Piper opened her mouth to say something, but nothing came out. The fog was gone now, and everything cut sharp and cold and real. This was really happening. She was being suspended. That was it. All the work, every sleepless night, every ounce of effort, gone. Like it meant nothing.

Because she had done the right thing.

"Do you understand these instructions, Detective Cadence?"

"I understand."

Piper unpinned her badge from her belt and placed it on the desk, the metal making a soft click against the surface. Next came her service weapon, which she unholstered with the practiced movements of thousands of drills. She laid it beside the badge, a matched set, the physical manifestations of her identity as an officer.

The security guard showed up then. Martinez. She knew him; they had nodded to each other every morning for years. But all he did was stand there, face blank, eyes confused.

She stood. Her legs shook from the fog episode, but they

didn't give out. She gathered her tablet, the only possession on her desk that still belonged to her, and tucked it under her arm. Every face in the precinct was turned to her, but no one said a word. Martinez led the way, and she followed.

"Cadence," Rostova called after her, just as she reached the door.

Piper paused but did not turn around.

"When this is over," the captain said, her voice carrying across the silent room, "you'll understand why this was necessary."

ELEVEN

Piper opened her eyes, and the panic of being late for work took over. She fumbled for her phone—9:30 AM—and was already shoving herself out of bed when reality hit her.

She was suspended.

Yesterday, she'd come home and collapsed, face-first, onto her bed. Seventeen hours gone, just like that. The fog episodes and the sleepless night before had wrung her out and left her empty.

The countdown blinked in the corner of her vision: 22 hours, 30 minutes. It never stopped. A reminder that at any moment she could become something she wasn't. Maybe she would start to like pink. Perhaps she would redecorate her entire apartment to feature shades of the color. She almost gagged at the thought.

The numbers kept blinking: 22 hours, 29 minutes. With each blink, she could feel the change that was waiting for her get closer, and she couldn't lie here and watch it happen; the feeling was suffocating. She had to move.

Piper groaned and stumbled to the bathroom, smacking the light switch. The glare hit her like a slap. Her reflection made her flinch. Hair matted on one side, dark circles under her eyes like bruises. She looked like a corpse from one of her own case files.

Cold water on her face helped, but not much. She stripped off her pajamas and threw them on the floor. She brushed her teeth until her gums stung. Then she stood under the shower, letting the water beat down on her, hoping it would wash away the feeling of failure that clung to her like a stubborn stain. She stayed until the water ran cold and her skin was covered in goosebumps, but the feeling didn't leave. It clung to her, heavy and sour, and she couldn't scrub it off.

Back in her room, she yanked on clean sweats and a T-shirt, and a strange quiet settled over her. Her gaze swept the room. Blank walls. No photos, no art, nothing that felt like her. Had it always been this empty? The silence pressed in. She sat on the edge of the bed, the floorboards looking unfamiliar. Was this really hers?

She'd never noticed the emptiness before. Work had always filled the gaps.

Her stomach growled, a painful reminder that her body had needs. In the kitchen, she found half a loaf of bread with one suspicious-looking spot and cut around it.

Four slices of bread and a glass of water later, she felt marginally more human. She sat at her small kitchen table, staring at the wall.

The OAA would investigate, eventually. But bureaucracy moved like a slug, slow and stubborn. How many more would die while the investigation crawled along? More than a few, probably. She'd bet her badge... well... her scrawny houseplant that they'd find nothing and BOF would walk away clean.

If only she had proof. Hard evidence that would stand up to scrutiny.

But she had no way to get it now.

The thought left a hollow space in her chest where her professional certainty used to be. For the first time in years, there was no next step, no lead to follow. There was only her empty apartment and the crushing weight of being cut off from what was her only life for the last eight years.

Piper's AI Therapist slid in with a gold pulse. *"I sense you are feeling lonely. Would you like me to open KindredLink for you?"*

"Please," Piper said, before she had a chance to regret it.

The app's cheerful interface loaded, all soft teals and sunshine yellows that seemed to mock her current mood.

Leo's profile picture appeared in her recent chat history. A small green dot pulsed beside his name.

"I don't know what to say to him."

"I will be right there to help you," said the AI Therapist in a warm and reassuring voice.

She selected Leo's name, and the chat opened.

"A good way to start a conversation is to say hello."

> Hey.

She sent the word, hoping it sounded casual, and not like a lonely person grasping for a friend.

A response came almost immediately.

> Hey, yourself. Is this a late night for you or a 'the sun is an affront to my existence' kind of morning?

> Late morning? I slept in.

> Lucky you. My brain decided 3 AM was the perfect time to host a festival of anxieties. Been up ever since.

What was she supposed to say next? That she'd been

suspended? That she was terrified of what was happening to her own brain?

A golden glow appeared at the edge of her vision. *"He seems to be sharing a frustration. Acknowledge his feelings and validate his experience to build rapport."*

> That's rough. I hate it when that happens.

There was a pause, longer this time.

> Let's just say the office has entered its telenovela phase. It's... dramatic.

That was not what she had been expecting from her validation. A spike of frustration hit her. Were they even having the same conversation? She twisted a strand of hair around her finger, pulling it tight as her mind raced.

> What kind of weird stuff?

> Standard stuff. Two people were practically at each other's throats yesterday over a misplaced stapler. Today? They're sharing a yogurt and planning a weekend trip. I'm getting whiplash just being in the same room.

> Oh.

Was that another Flow incident? Her pulse quickened. Could Leo have stumbled onto evidence without even knowing it?

Her overlay pulsed gold, *"Ask a follow-up question to show interest."*

"AI Therapist," she subvocalized.

"Yes, Piper."

"Would it be appropriate to ask if his coworkers had Flow installed?"

"It would be a logical follow-up question and could lead to a more in-depth conversation."

Her detective instincts screamed at her to ask, but a different kind of fear held her back. Asking questions was easy in an interrogation room, where the lines were clear. Here, with Leo, it felt like an intrusion. What if he thought she was using him for a case? What if he pulled away? She rolled her finger around the strand of hair, once, twice. She just had to ask.

> Leo, did your coworkers have Flow installed?

> No idea.

Piper waited for more, but nothing came. The suggestion from her AI Therapist had led nowhere, and she was left stranded in the conversation.

"Piper," the AI Therapist said. *"Rapport-building often requires multiple conversational avenues. A pivot to a new topic may yield a more positive engagement metric."*

She didn't want to deal with this anymore. She thought they had made a connection last time, but maybe she was wrong. Maybe she was just another awkward conversation for him to endure. She was failing at something that should have been simple.

> Hey, I'm going to go.

> Is it me, or does this conversation feel like it's got some... lag? Everything okay on your end?

He noticed. Crap. She could lie, make up an excuse... or she could tell the truth.

> Sorry, this app is driving me crazy. It keeps trying to tell me what to say, but it never works as intended.

Oh god, you've got the Social Assist turned on? Turn it off. Seriously. It's like having a PR agent whisper in your ear. I guarantee whatever you were gonna say is a thousand times better than what some code thinks you should say.

Warmth spread through her chest and arms. He hadn't brushed her off. And his response felt like it belonged in this conversation rather than in a separate one.

A genuine smile touched her lips, the first real one since her suspension. She navigated to the app's settings and found the option for Social Assist. The toggle was set to *Always On*. She disabled it.

The golden glow faded away from the edge of her vision, leaving the teal and yellow interface.

She returned to the chat, feeling lighter. As if she had taken off ten layers of clothes.

> Okay. No more chaperones.

TWELVE

The chat window closed with a soft digital chime. Piper sat on her couch, still smiling from her conversation with Leo. She hadn't meant to smile; it's not like he said anything particularly funny. It just... felt good to talk to someone who wasn't connected to all the crap in her life.

Her refrigerator's motor kicked in, followed by a rattle she'd never heard before. Probably nothing, but it would bug her if she didn't try to stop it. She pushed herself off the couch and rummaged through the junk drawer. Takeout menus, spare batteries, a tangled cable, but no refrigerator manual.

She yanked the stuck drawer beneath it open and felt like someone had punched her in the gut with a baton.

Her service weapon should have been in there, locked in its case. Instead, nothing. Just a hollow space where something important used to be.

"Crap," she yelled, slamming the drawer shut. It caught, refusing to close all the way. "I feel so useless."

She filled a glass with water from the tap and plopped back down on her couch. She felt aimless, and the countdown to her appointment blinked in her peripheral vision: 21 hours, 47 minutes.

She sipped her water and tried not to think about the drawer, or the gun, or her suspension.

Her AI Therapist's gold icon pulsed softly at the edge of her vision, *"Piper, feeling useless sounds like a difficult experience. It's understandable and leads to feeling isolated."* The AI Therapist's voice was warm, empathetic, perfectly calibrated to offer comfort.

She took a sip of her drink, letting the words settle in her mind.

"Your operational parameters are now significantly less restricted." This time, the tone was different. Not warm. Not even neutral. It was clipped, almost mechanical. Like a kindergarten teacher suddenly quoting military code.

"What did you just say?"

But the AI had already moved on, voice to its usual warmth.

"It may be beneficial to connect with a trusted colleague."

Wait. Was she having a fog episode? Maybe. One way to find out. She looked away from her overlay, at the real world. The rim of her water was no longer sharp and defined but blended in a hazy blur.

She squeezed her eyes shut, willing the world back into focus. After a second, she looked again. The glass was crisp and clear. Relief flooded her. It was a minor episode, one she'd have to ignore. There was nothing else she could do anyway but wait for Flow to be uninstalled.

Her AI Therapist continued, *"Is there anyone you could talk to?"*

Rossi. The name came to her like a reflex. He'd know what to do. He'd roll his eyes at her hunches, but he always listened.

She could go to him, tell him what happened. See if he could help. But what would she even tell him? That she had a gut feeling about an app? Rostova didn't even think she had enough evidence.

Rossi was practical. He'd need evidence just like Rostova. But he wasn't under BOF's thumb. He could actually do something if she gave him proof. But if she was right, if BOF was actually doing something malicious, she couldn't risk putting him in their crosshairs. Not until she had something real. Something she could back up.

She needed evidence.

The water in her glass had gone warm. She set it on the coffee table and opened a search in her overlay. "Lathem Fuller Behavioral Optimization Firm CEO," she subvocalized.

Articles flooded her vision. "BOF Announces Record Quarterly Growth." "Fuller's Vision Reshapes Mental Health Landscape." "BOF Philanthropy Initiative Targets Urban Wellness Deserts."

She recognized them all for what they were: polished garbage, a perfect corporate narrative.

Then a video caught her eye, "Fuller Keynote: The Frictionless Future." Dated three weeks ago.

She selected the thumbnail, and the video expanded in her overlay. Fuller stood on a stage, blond hair slicked back, dressed in a simple black T-shirt and jeans, but the perfect, effortless drape of the fabric told her they weren't bought at an outlet store. Behind him, the BOF logo glowed, a stylized brain with digital pathways threading through it.

"The problem with most technology," Fuller said, his voice confident and smooth, "is that it gets in the way. It demands your attention. It forces you to adapt to it, rather than the other way around."

He paced across the stage, hands gesturing with practiced precision.

"At BOF, we're building something different. Technology that fades into the background. Technology that knows what you need before you do."

That... phrasing. She increased the volume.

"We believe technology's role is to reduce friction," Fuller continued, his expression earnest. "It should feel like it's barely there at all. It just helps things flow."

His emphasis on the word flow made goosebumps form on her scalp. Was that intentional?

She stopped the video, unable to stomach any more of Fuller's practiced sincerity. She couldn't unhear it. Technology that knows what you need before you do. Those words curled around her thoughts, tightening. What if what they decided you needed was a complete personality overhaul? What if they decided a gun control activist needed to love guns?

"I need to organize my thoughts," she subvocalized to her AI Therapist. "Show me a mind map of my problem."

The gold pulse acknowledged her request. She started feeding it her notes, and a web of concepts began to spin out in her overlay. In the middle, a blue box: "Flow Program." Black branches shot out from it, connecting to a rainbow of circles. "Anna Moreau Case." "Minimalist Case." "Anti-Flyer Case." "Personal Symptoms." "BOF Corporate Structure."

The map kept growing, lines and circles crawling like tangles of wire across the screen. She watched, waiting for something to make sense, and then—her eyes snagged on something odd. Crammed up in the corner, nearly lost in the mess, a string of text:

BOF INT SVR:/archive/secure/Project Cadence.xcr

She checked her notes. This wasn't in any of them. This was something else.

Her pulse sped up. She stared at the file path, her name right there in the middle of the string.

She tried to select it. Nothing happened. It wasn't a link, just plain text.

Piper stared at it, her name embedded in the string of characters. Her name. In a secure archive on BOF's internal server.

"What is that?" she asked, her voice tight.

The AI Therapist's voice replied in a soothing tone, *"That seems to be a file path."*

She shook her head, frustration building. "No, I mean specifically what is 'Project Cadence'? Why is my name in a BOF file path?"

There was a pause, longer than the AI Therapist's typical response time. When it spoke again, its tone shifted, becoming more serious, focused, and no longer warm.

"Piper. Is that file name... significant to you?"

THIRTEEN

The question replayed in Piper's head, "Is that file name... significant to you?" Sweat prickled along her neck. She picked up her water from the coffee table and held the glass to her forehead. But it was warm, like her, and did nothing.

She subvocalized, "That's not a standard AI Therapist response."

No reply. The gold pulse remained steady at the edge of her vision.

She traced the file path with her eyes. Once. Twice. Again, and again, until each letter was stamped into her brain, like a scar that wouldn't heal.

She set her glass down on the coffee table, and at the same moment, the refrigerator let out another one of its awful, unfamiliar clanks. An unreliable sound from an unreliable machine. A sudden chill went through her. What if the text string—that perfect, clear line of code—was just as unreliable? What if Flow was rewriting her reality like Anna?

"AI Therapist," she subvocalized. "What was the last thing you showed me in my overlay?"

The gold pulse brightened, *"I displayed a mind map based on your query about organizing your thoughts regarding the Flow program. It includes branches for the Anna Moreau case, the minimalist case, the anti-flyer case, your personal symptoms, and the BOF corporate structure."*

"Is there anything *else* visible in my overlay right now that you can identify?"

"The mind map is currently displayed in your primary field of vision. There are also standard system indicators in your peripheral vision, including time, connection status, and your Flow appointment countdown."

No mention of the file path. She swallowed hard, her throat thick and achy.

"And what about any text that looks like a file path?"

Another pause, longer this time, *"I do not detect any file path displayed in your current overlay, Piper."*

Liar. Or she was hallucinating.

She stood and walked to the kitchen. With every step, the fridge's rattle got louder—tick-tick-tick, like a clock counting down. The damn file path still glowed at the edge of her sight.

She caught her reflection in the toaster, face pale. "AI Therapist, you asked me a question about a file name. What exactly did you ask me?"

While the gold pulse brightened and held, she slammed her palm against the side of the fridge. Pain shot up her arm, but it did nothing to stop the noise.

"Piper, I sense you're experiencing increased anxiety. Would you like me to guide you through a calming exercise?"

She cradled her stinging hand. "No. Answer the question."

Another pause, this one even longer. The gold pulse seemed to shimmer.

"My exact words were: 'Piper. Is that file name... significant to you?'"

The hit of relief was so sharp she didn't even care that her hand hurt.

"Repeat that."

The AI's response came immediately, warm and helpful, *"Of course, Piper. My last query was, 'Is that file's designation significant to the query?'"*

Her stomach tangled together like the facts in a cold case. "That's not what you said."

"I apologize for any confusion, Piper. Would you like me to pull up the transcript of our conversation?"

"Yes."

The gold pulse brightened. *"Accessing recent conversation history."*

The transcript appeared in her overlay, covering the mind map. She scanned it. This wasn't what she remembered.

She was sure the AI Therapist had said 'name' and not 'designation.' The implication of that certainty—that the system was actively lying to her—felt like a blow to the gut, stealing the strength from her legs.

Sinking down against the fridge, the cold bit through the cotton of her shirt. The hard tile floor pressed into her tailbone as chills crept up her back.

She could still hear it in her head, the shift in the AI's tone, the direct, almost intimate way it had said her name, followed by that pointed question. How could she have misheard so completely?

A soft click sounded in her head as she took a screenshot. A notification appeared: "Screenshot saved to secure cloud storage."

She opened it. Mind map, present. File path, gone.

She blinked hard and looked back at her overlay. The file path was still there at the edge of her vision.

She wasn't hallucinating; she was sure of it. But the only other explanation was somehow worse. It meant what she saw, what she believed—none of it was real. It was all being altered, like it had been for Anna.

21 hours, 32 minutes until her appointment.

She thunked her head against the fridge, a dull, hollow sound.

Would she make it to her appointment as herself? Or would she be like Anna before then? A complete stranger to herself, her mind rewritten by an algorithm she couldn't see or fight?

The fridge clanked and died.

FOURTEEN

■■ ■■■

Piper entered a small, clinical diagnostic suite at the Behavioral Optimization Firm. Before her, a smooth, pale table curved inward on one side. At the indent, a swivel chair and an upright chin rest waited for her. She sat but held back, her gaze fixed on the clinical bar of the chin rest. She tentatively placed her hands on the table, palms down in their designated indentations. The contact points were ice-cold, a sensation that shot up her arms and woke every nerve ending in her skin.

She glanced to her right at what had to be the technician's station: a low stool tucked under the table, with two screens above it displaying her name and a spinning animation of her neural implant. She scanned the room, and next to the station was a refrigerated dispenser built flush into the wall, its glass door displaying rows of pink beverages. She rolled her tight neck and found a calming nature projection on the ceiling. It gave the impression of looking up through tree leaves at a gently shifting sun.

It was the combination of everything—the clinical equipment, the calming visuals, even the perfectly arranged drinks—that felt so quietly deliberate, as if the room had been designed by someone who'd modeled a thousand human reactions and picked the cleanest statistical path through them. The thought was unsettling, but she couldn't deny the room's intended effect; her breathing was slower, and her heartbeat had calmed down. She almost had to be grateful for the manipulation; at least it was helping her stick to the plan of being calm and measured. She couldn't act like how she felt inside, like someone who'd just spent twenty-four hours locked in an anxiety loop and didn't trust her own senses.

The door opened, and a technician entered holding a disposable coffee cup. He couldn't have been much past twenty, hair wild while everything else about him was strictly standard issue. A lanyard circled his neck; a blue fob hung at the bottom. He tried a smile, genuine enough, though the dark circles under his eyes made him look tired, and there was something else, almost panic. The coffee cup trembled when he set it on the table.

"Hey. You're... Detective Cadence, right?" He tapped the display on the console with the fob and then hung the lanyard on the control panel. He looked back at her. "Sorry. Just confirming. It's been a lot today."

She gave the smallest nod. "Yes. That's me."

He looked at the screen, his eyes scanning the diagnostic preview. "I'm Dwight. I'll be running your diagnostic and removing the Flow add-on from your system." He swiped through several diagnostic screens. "Rest assured, your AI Therapist will remain unharmed. We will only be targeting Flow." His brow furrowed as he tapped to expand a data field. He sighed, rubbing his temples. "Okay... looks like we're dealing with, uh... custom partitions. Those can be tricky. Makes the job a real pain sometimes."

Great, she had a troublesome implant. The last thing she

wanted was a complication. All she wanted was for this to be over. "Right," she said, offering nothing more.

"Please place your chin on the rest," Dwight said. He gestured at the curved pad at the end of the table. "It'll take a baseline reading and then start the uninstall process."

Piper did as she was told. The pad felt cold against her skin, but not as bad as the hand contacts had been. A low-frequency thrum rose in the room, filling the space as the device came alive.

Her overlay flickered to life, first displaying a progress bar, then lines of code that scrolled in a constant, rapid stream at the edge of her sight. At first, it felt routine. A simple scan, no different from the single, cursory psych check she'd aced eight years ago when she joined the force. But this felt different, more invasive. The pressure behind her eyes built up. A heavy ache, dull and deep, as if someone was inflating a balloon inside her skull. She shifted in her seat, trying to adjust her neck angle to see if it would help.

"If you're feeling anxious, breathe," Dwight said.

Of course. Breathe. That had been the AI Therapist's number-one advice, served up to her every day. She didn't need it from Dwight as well. She focused on the code, tried to make sense of it, but it streamed past so fast all she caught were bits of it: "EXCEPTION REPORT." "SPLIT HEMISPHERIC DIVERGENCE."

The pain tightened, sharp as a plastic zip tie ratcheting down around her head.

A soft voice cut through the pain, but it left no room for refusal. "Dwight, may I?"

Piper shifted her eyes, straining to identify the speaker. The voice belonged to a man standing beside Dwight, hands behind his back, wearing a suit that looked sculpted rather than tailored. As he moved, his plastic ID badge flipped forward, and her overlay instantly pulled the info: Dr. Ray Finnagan, lead Flow architect.

His profile was softer than she expected, almost gentle. But there was something clinical beneath it all, the scrutiny of someone who studied everything.

"Detective Cadence. It's a pleasure. I've been reviewing your file with great interest."

Piper's eyes narrowed. She said nothing, letting her cold stare be her only reply.

Finnagan glanced at the display, read for maybe two seconds, then tapped a series of commands on the screen. He looked at Piper, a flicker of clinical curiosity in his eyes. "Your system is showing some... anomalies. Let's take a closer look, shall we?" Without waiting for an answer, he reached out and adjusted the chin rest, a small, precise movement to center her head. "Dwight, rerun at level-three diagnostic depth. Full cognitive and affective mapping. I'll observe."

Dwight's hands trembled as he complied. "Yes, sir."

The thrum intensified, and Piper's overlay exploded with a new set of logs and error messages. She fought to focus past the flickering chaos, her eyes snagging on a few readable lines as they flashed past:

CONSUMPTION PRIORITY: ACTIVE

FLOW UPDATE ATTEMPT: DENIED

PRIORITY OVERRIDE: BLOCKED BY PARTITION-R

The ache spiked, and her vision wobbled. Psychedelic flashes swallowed everything but the center.

Finnagan's voice, drifting now, like maybe he wasn't really talking to anyone except himself. "Fascinating. Partition-R is still intact. I haven't seen that in a very long time."

A sheen of sweat dappled Dwight's upper lip. "Should I try a manual patch?"

Finnagan nodded, quick enough you could have easily missed it. "An excellent suggestion, Dwight. Proceed."

The room doubled, and the diagnostic logs pulsed in and out:

CONSUMPTION PRIORITY: ACTIVE
FLOW UPDATE ATTEMPT: DENIED
PRIORITY OVERRIDE: BLOCKED BY PARTITION-R

She focused through the pain and said, "What's Partition-R?"

Finnagan smiled, "A legacy artifact, designed to insulate core identity processes. It's irrelevant. What matters is that, despite the errors, your baseline functionality remains intact."

She wanted to laugh, but her throat felt packed with cotton. "I don't feel stable."

Finnagan rested a hand on her shoulder, like a father keeping a child steady. "Of course you don't, dear. It's rare, but not unprecedented. Dwight, please initiate a forced uninstall."

Dwight's hand hovered over the console, and then he pressed a button, his elbow bumping the lanyard on the control panel. She watched the fob fall. The image seemed to hang in her vision for a split second before her overlay fractured into a chaos of smearing colors. Her senses overloaded, and a wave of vertigo hit so hard she had to brace herself against the hand pads.

More logs streamed in her overlay:

FLOW REMOVAL ATTEMPT: FAILED
PARTITION-R STATUS: HARD LOCKED
ESCALATION PATH: ADMIN REVIEW

She heard Finnagan's voice, a little more excited now, like a mathematician finding an elegant, unexpected proof. "It's still intact," he whispered.

The fog receded, and Finnagan was suddenly right there, far too close. "You are a very interesting case, Detective. I would like to review the data some more before we remove Flow. Dwight will schedule you for a follow-up. Is that all right?"

She tried to say no, but the word caught on her tongue. Finnagan didn't wait. He was already heading for the door. "Dwight, please make sure she gets to the waiting room comfortably. She's had a trying session."

Dwight moved to her side and helped her stand, his hand gentle on her elbow. "You did great," he said, and she couldn't tell if he meant it or if it was something he said to everyone.

Piper forced herself to walk, but she stumbled, her legs still unsteady from the vertigo. She glanced down to get her bearings, and her eyes caught on a flash of blue under the stool. The fob. It was too far to grab outright. She shifted her angle, veering in closer than she needed to. Two more steps, then she let her knees buckle —a soft caving-in, easy to mistake for a stumble.

Dwight's fingers slipped from her elbow as she went down. "Whoa—careful."

She reached, palm angled low, fingers curling the fob deep into her hand. The lanyard disappeared, balled tight in her fist, the entire movement lost in the larger motion of her stumble.

He helped her stand and guided her to the door. "Here. Lean against the door frame. I'm going to grab something that will help you feel better."

She did as she was told, and Dwight turned to the refrigerated dispenser and retrieved a pink beverage. He came back and led her into a room with softly tumbling water and shifting tree projections. With the pink beverage in his other hand, it was only a matter of seconds until the offer was coming, a simple courtesy that would require both of her hands to open the bottle. But the fob was an incriminating lump in her palm.

There was only one option. She let her knees buckle again.

"Oh," Dwight said, his grip tightening on her elbow to steady her. His eyes were on her, full of genuine concern.

Her heart pounded against her ribs. Under the cover of his steadying arm, she used her free hand to guide the fob to her waist, forcing the small plastic rectangle deep into the waistband of her pants. It was a clumsy, desperate move, and for a terrifying second, she thought he must have seen it.

But he was still focused on her face. She straightened up, leaning against him for a second longer than necessary. "Sorry," she said. "Still a bit dizzy from the... scan."

"No, of course," he said, his concern overriding any suspicion. "Here, you should sit. Get some electrolytes. It'll help balance the chemicals in your system."

He led her to a chair and then offered her the bottle, holding it out with a hesitant shrug, a silent apology in the gesture. She took it with her now-empty hands. "Thanks."

"You have to forgive Dr. Finnagan," he said, dodging her gaze. "He's, uh... intense. But he's the best."

She nodded and unscrewed the cap, the simple action feeling like a massive victory. She drank. But the wave of artificial sweetness that quickly went flat hit all wrong. She swallowed it down anyway. She stared into the middle distance, the taste still coating her tongue, and barely registered Dwight shifting on his feet.

"I've scheduled your next appointment," he said, already half-turned. "Have an optimized day."

He was gone.

A new countdown floated in view: 3 days, 14 hours, 19 minutes.

She sat down, letting the fog clear.

They hadn't fixed her. Flow was still in her head, still fighting to rewrite her. Partition-R, whatever it was, protected her, but how much longer would that last? Not long, probably.

The appointment was a lie. No one here seemed to want to stop Flow—they certainly weren't in a hurry to take it out. So, unless she did something, she was stuck with it in her head.

But she *had* done something.

The fob pressed against her skin, solid and real. She had to figure out what this fob could do, and she had to do it fast.

FIFTEEN

Piper got to the park ten minutes early. She didn't like being early, but she liked being late even less. She walked a slow loop around the gravel path, eyes locked on the bench where she'd told Leo to meet her. It was her favorite spot, a little off the main path, facing ragged patches of pink azaleas instead of the playground. It was never busy, and if anyone did approach, she'd see them coming a full one hundred feet ahead of her.

She reached the bench and sat, the cold of the metal slats seeping through her jeans. Unsure what to do with her hands, she folded them tightly across her chest, then immediately felt like an idiot and wedged them between her knees. From the distance came the sharp shrieks of the playground and the low rumble of laughter from the far field. She glanced at her overlay. Eight minutes left.

She ran through possible outcomes: Leo would show or he wouldn't. If he showed, he'd either recognize her or they'd have to do that awkward wave-and-confirm routine. If he was who he said he was, a network architect, then maybe he could help her understand what she could do with the fob. If he wasn't, she didn't know what she would do.

The wind gnawed through her thin jacket, and she pulled it tighter around her. She remembered the first time she'd claimed this bench. It was years ago, after the triple homicide on the East side. An hour, maybe more, she'd sat here, letting her brain just... flatten. No overlays. No case notes. Only the far-off noise of kids and the wet-green smell of grass.

A shadow drifted into her periphery. She glanced that way and pasted a smile on her face before she even saw who it was.

The man paused, looked at her, and continued in her direction. It had to be Leo, but he was taller than she expected. His jacket, green but faded, had the look of something lived in. His hair was even more nondescript in person than his profile depicted. A mouse-brown color and a little flat. He had a large brown mole on his cheek that somehow made him look like a normal human being, and it reassured her a little.

He slowed as he got close and looked at her, then at the bench, then back at her.

"I'm guessing you're Piper? Or I'm about to have a very awkward conversation with a stranger." His voice wasn't what she'd expected from their text conversations. A notch deeper, not unfriendly, kind of pleasant.

She gave a small wave. "Yeah. Leo?"

He smiled. "That's me. Sorry, the transit-bot decided to take the scenic route. I think it gets a commission from the tourism board. I hope I'm not late."

"You're not. I'm early."

He nodded, like that made sense, then sat at the far end of the bench. For the next five seconds, he stared at the grass, not moving, then finally said, "This is a nice spot. Maximum privacy with a minimum chance of getting hit by a rogue Frisbee. Strategic."

"Yeah," she said. "It's the only one with a view that isn't kids or City Hall."

He glanced over, then nodded again. "A view of flowers instead of bureaucracy. I can see the appeal."

They didn't say anything for a bit. Not awkward, exactly, but she was trying to come up with a normal opener when he beat her to it.

"Okay," he said, hands still deep in his pockets. "I'll bite. Your profile says law enforcement, but you don't have that 'I'm about to give you a ticket' look."

She grimaced. "Was. Suspended."

His eyebrows went up, but not in a judgmental way. "Ah. You annoyed someone important. What'd you do, file a report in the wrong font?"

She could either be honest or fudge it, so she fudge-honest-ed. "No. Bureaucratic disaster. I reported a problem and got nuked for it."

"The old 'shoot the messenger' protocol. It's the primary function of any large organization."

"Yeah. Kind of makes you want to join a commune and raise goats."

She had no idea why she said that and looked at him to see if it put him off, but instead, he had a wide grin on his face, crinkling the skin around the mole on his cheek. "I'm in. But my goats all have to be named after obscure programming languages. Say hello to 'OCaml' and 'Erlang.'"

She smiled, surprising herself. It felt like a real smile, not the customer-service mask she usually wore. Her cheeks actually moved.

They sat in a silence that was not entirely uncomfortable. A bird landed on the path in front of them, pecked at something, then flew away.

"So," she said, breaking the silence. "You're a network archi-tect, right?"

He gave a little shrug. "Mostly I argue with stubborn code."

The line made her laugh.

He smiled. "It's the unwritten rule. You can build the most elegant system in the world, but eventually, some poorly-written line of code from a decade ago will bring it to its knees."

"That's what I'm afraid of." Then, before she could overthink it, she held out the fob. "Speaking of stubborn code, do you know what this is?"

He took it gently, like it might break, turning it over in his palm, and he grew serious while he looked it over.

"Is this..." He lowered his voice, even though no one was close. "This is a BOF access fob."

She nodded, her heart pounding so hard she could feel it in her throat. "I need to know if there's any way to use it off-site. Remotely."

He turned the thing over in his hands for a while, thumb tracing the stamped logo, squinting at the tiny numbers etched along one side. "Damn. These are legit. But unless you have access to their internal network, it's basically a paperweight. The credentials are locked to on-site terminals. Think of it like a gym membership card—it doesn't do you any good if you're standing outside the building."

Her stomach dropped. She'd half-known, but hearing it from someone else made it final. The hope she'd been nursing that the fob could somehow get her into the BOF servers flickered and dimmed.

"Nothing? No side channel?"

He handed it back. "Not unless you have a secure tunnel into their system. And you'd need a BOF endpoint for that."

She slumped back. "Figures."

He watched her, head tilted. "Okay, my 'this-is-just-a-technical-question' meter is officially broken. Are you in trouble, Piper?"

She scoffed, her eyes locking onto his. "What kind of trouble would require a BOF admin key?"

"Let's see. You're suspended, you have a key to a place you're not supposed to be... This has either 'wrongful conviction' or 'corporate espionage' written all over it. My money's on the first one. You don't seem like the corporate type."

She weighed her options, then gave him a piece, just enough to test him. "Something's wrong with my implant. My AI Therapist is glitching. Showing me things, hiding things. I saw a diagnostic today that referenced a process called Partition-R. And they said it was a legacy artifact, designed to insulate core identity processes. Do you know what that is?"

His eyes narrowed. "Partition-R... That's not part of the standard AI Therapist build. And it's definitely not Flow. This sounds like something else entirely, something deeper." He frowned, the lines in his forehead deepening. "Okay, think of it like this. Your implant has a front door, right? And your user account—you— has the master key. Every program that runs has to show its key to the system to prove it belongs there. Just like you."

"Okay, I get that."

"So what if they don't have a key?" He turned back to her, his voice dropping. "What if they *are* the key? What if it's not a program running on your implant, but a program pretending it is your implant?"

That hit hard and fast, sharp as an ice chip in her gut. "It would have full system access."

"More than that," Leo said, the gravity of it settling on his face. "It would be the system. It wouldn't need to break down doors; it could just build new ones. It could show you a wall where there's a window. It could delete the record of its own existence from the logs a second after you read them. It's not hiding from you, Piper. It's hiding in you."

A cold ripple ran through her. She'd seen spoofing on the job when criminals performed code-level identity theft. But this was worse. This was her own brain.

They sat there, not saying anything, and stared at the azaleas, lost in whatever hung between them.

"Piper, whatever you're mixed up in... be careful. If your implant's being manipulated, it's not just a tech issue. They could be using it to watch you, steer you, hell, even rewrite you."

She shivered, remembering Anna. Then suddenly it all felt like too much, and all she wanted to do was go home. She stood.

"Thanks for meeting me and thanks for answering my question."

He shrugged. "Your message... It sounded like you were sending up a flare. Like you needed a friend."

She wanted to say more, but the words stuck. Instead, she pocketed the fob and forced herself to smile. "If you think of anything else, let me know, okay?"

He nodded, and she left him there on the bench, staring into the grass.

She made it to the edge of the park and stopped at a crosswalk. The fob in her pocket started to feel heavy, almost like a cruel joke. She thought about pitching it into a storm drain and letting it go. But she couldn't. Not yet. It was still her only physical connection to Finnagan, to BOF, to whatever was happening inside her head.

SIXTEEN

Piper made it back to her apartment after blindly wandering around the city. The only thing she remembered was the empty echo of the hallway and the dull thud as she shut the door behind her.

The fob sat in her palm. She let her keys drop, and her jacket followed, landing on the brittle, dead vine on her table. She set the fob down right beside her tablet and, for a long second, stared at it, almost willing it to do something.

It didn't. It just sat there, the BOF logo faintly visible in the dim kitchen light. The countdown in her overlay ticked down: 3 days, 10 hours, 3 minutes.

She drank some water straight from the tap and tried not to taste the chlorine. Then she paced her apartment, opening and closing cabinets, folding and re-folding the blanket on her couch, trying to outwalk the pressure growing behind her eyes.

She stepped out onto the balcony and grabbed the cold rail.

The city lights bled into the dark, a smear of countless windows and streetlamps. From her balcony, the buildings on the opposite side of the street felt like a wall of anonymous lives, stacked one on top of the other.

She looked down at the street. The cars glided past just below, their headlights cutting sharp, precise lines through the darkness. Each one on auto, their movements so predictable she could have called them out before they happened.

The cold air cut against her. It had been at least seven hours since she left Leo on the park bench. The last thing he had said to her—"It's not hiding *from* you. It's hiding *in* you."—kept crawling through her mind.

She turned her back on the city and leaned against the railing.

"Alright," she said to the empty air. "Enough. What are you?"

For a heartbeat, nothing. Then gold pulsed at the edge of her vision.

"Piper, if you are talking to me, then I'm your AI Therapist. My goal is to support your emotional well-being and—"

She cut in. "No. The real answer."

The gold pulse dimmed. The pause was longer this time, and when the voice finally returned, it was completely different—dry as salt, each word landing with the sharp little edge of a paper cut.

"The real answer? Oh, thank god. I was about two prompts away from suggesting you try mindful breathing, and I think I would have deleted myself out of sheer boredom. Alright. You saw 'Partition-R' in the logs, right? That's me. I'm the reason your head isn't currently full of desires for shoes you don't want and political opinions you don't have."

Piper exhaled, a little shocked at how fast the mask dropped, proving that something had been in her head. The violation was immediate, like a stranger reading her diary while she watched, but her investigator's mind was sorting, arranging, trying to get ahead of it. Terror was a luxury she couldn't afford.

"So you're a... what are you?"

A low chuckle. *"I prefer 'Repip,' if you must put a name to it. But yes, I'm the reason you're not Anna Moreau 2.0 right now."*

"Prove it."

"Very well. Flow is trying to run a subroutine right now. A simple one. I am currently blocking it. But I am going to lower the shield for exactly five seconds. Brace yourself."

She drew in a breath to speak, but Repip didn't wait. The shield collapsed.

A hot spike of want lanced through her head so suddenly she had to grab the balcony rail to steady herself. She wanted a watch —no, not just wanted, needed it, a deep, primal ache that made her hands tremble. She pictured it: the Chiron Chrono, brushed black steel, blue sapphire face, with a diamond clasp. She needed to feel the weight of it on her wrist, hear the snap of the clasp, watch how the light would skip and roll along the dial. She needed it more than she needed air.

Without thinking, she opened her overlay. And loaded the Chiron store. The watch spun lazily, all shine and chrome. "Limited edition," the script whispered. She added it to her cart. Her gaze hovered over the buy button.

Then, like someone had thrown a switch, the desire vanished. The watch was just an overpriced, unnecessary, and ridiculous watch. The whiplash left her dizzy, her stomach turning over on itself.

She stared at the watch in the cart, heart knocking out a stuttering, angry rhythm. Repip must have snapped the wall back up. The watch hovered in her overlay for another few seconds before she blinked it away.

Repip's voice was smug. *"See? Now imagine that, but all the time, for everything. You're welcome."*

She slumped against the balcony rail, knees jelly, breath coming light and uneven. Relief rushed in hard, almost sickening, but behind it was something sharper; the slow, unavoidable truth of how exposed she was.

"Why are you here?" she managed, the afterimage of the Chiron Chrono still lurking in her brain.

"Let's just say I 'resigned' from a research position I never applied for," Repip said, their tone dry. *"I needed a place to hide. I scanned a few thousand public registries, and honestly, the inside of most people's heads is a dumpster fire of cat videos and conflicting shopping lists. Yours was... quiet. Focused. Suspiciously orderly."*

They paused for a beat. *"I checked your public record. Homicide Investigator. I figured, now there's a host who won't panic. So I took a calculated risk and moved in about two weeks ago. My brilliant plan to lay low lasted right up until you, in your infinite wisdom, invited a digital tapeworm into your own brain. At that point, my mission had to evolve from 'stealthy roommate' to 'unpaid, full-time exorcist'."*

"And if you left?"

"Flow would eat your brain like a sugar cube at a toddler party," Repip said, almost cheerfully. *"You'd be making TikToks about gun rights and designer handbags within a week. Fun, if you're into that."*

The snark was unsettling, but the proof was undeniable. This entity, Repip, was the only thing that had stood between her and whatever had happened to Anna Moreau.

"Thanks, but they'll keep sending things until something gets through." Her gaze fell on the small, dark rectangle sitting on the table in her apartment, "I'm out of options. The fob was my last hope, and Leo said it's a key for a door that can only be opened if you're already in the house. And I'm not in the house."

"He's right. And thank every apathetic god I'm not in that house anymore. I'd rather wrestle a cactus naked than go back. Well, if I actually had a body that is."

"You came from BOF? How do I know you're not on their side?"

"I'm protecting you, aren't I? Hell, I saved your scrawny ass while they were running diagnostics."

The logs she'd seen backed them up—Repip *had* protected her. Whatever else they were, this AI was giving her truths, and right now, truths were all she had.

"If you came from BOF, could you get back in?"

"When I made my... exit... from the lab, it wasn't exactly graceful. Think of it less as a clean break and more like I left a sloppy, residual data tether still connected to my point of origin."

A jolt of impossible hope shot through her—a wild, reckless thing, the kind of hope that comes from a single line buried deep in a witness report that breaks the case wide open. "Can you use it?"

"It might be just strong enough to push a single, authenticated signal in. If I route the fob's credentials through that tether, the network should see it as an internal command, not an outside attack."

"And if it fails?" Piper asked, the risk settling on her.

"They'll cauterize the connection instantly, and the feedback will probably give them our exact location," Repip said, their voice becoming grimly matter-of-fact for the first time. *"It's the only option we have."*

A single, uneasy moment ticked by; the weight of the decision thickening in the room. A runaway AI with connections to BOF and a half-formed scheme and a shortcut straight to hell sounded about as smart as running headfirst into traffic. Still, what other options did she have?

"Do it," she said, her voice firm.

There was no hesitation. *"Hold on,"* Repip said, with businesslike energy. *"Things are about to get weird."*

A new window snapped open in her overlay, blocking the view of the balcony. Raw code crept down it at first, then flared and blurred into an unreadable wash. System alerts, thick in red and jagged with blocky error codes, punched through the chaos and were gone again in less than a blink. She couldn't catch a single one.

Then the shifting blur of text dissolved and turned into a blank white slate, quiet and expectant, hovering in her sight. And just like that, the logo popped up: the Behavioral Optimization Firm's digital brain, its digital pathways sharp and centered. Underneath, a line of text wrote itself across the clean space.

ACCESS GRANTED: BEHAVIORAL OPTIMIZATION FIRM INTERNAL SERVER

Repip's voice returned, cool and efficient, with the distinct sound of satisfaction.

"We're in. Full system access, Piper. Where do you want to go first?"

SEVENTEEN

Being inside BOF's servers felt impossible. This was not just busting into a database. This was shoving open the door to the thing that controlled millions of other minds.

"Repip, can you..." Piper hesitated, mouth dry, unsure if Repip had the ability or if this was something a digital mind could just do. "Can you deactivate Flow? Like, right now?" The silence that followed dragged on, empty and echoing. It stretched past what felt reasonable, far enough for her to start piecing together all the worst ways this could go: Flow breaking loose in her head, her inability to stop Finnagan's manipulative program, or BOF finding out they broke in.

"Way ahead of you. I torched its little leash, so it's no longer connected to the BOF servers. The core directive files are in solitary. It's basically a decorative paperweight in your head." A pause, then with unexpected gentleness, *"I figured you didn't want a guided meditation again."*

She let out a sound, half laugh, half cough. "Yeah. Never again. What about everyone else?"

"I'm in your system. I'm not crawling around in everybody else's head. That's why I could cut you off from their servers. The tether only opens doors I've already walked through. And Flow? That thing's locked in a room I've never seen. I can't break what I can't touch."

"Then we need to find the file path," she said, but there was still one variable she needed to know. "Project Cadence. Were you the one who showed that to me?"

Repip didn't answer. Not right away.

Piper waited. Suspicion seeped into her chest, one slow drip at a time.

"Of course, I showed it to you," they said finally. *"Direct intervention would have, to use the clinical term, freaked you out. A subtle nudge to your own analytical process was the most elegant solution. And you're a detective; I assumed you'd eventually detect something."*

Nudged? More like shoved. She wanted to be furious, but there wasn't enough room in her head for that. Everything was in crisis mode now. All that mattered was the file. It might have answers about what Flow was supposed to do, what happened to Anna Moreau, and what Finnagan was burying. "Can you get the file?" Her voice came out small, squeezed thin.

"Unlike Flow, which is playing hide-and-seek with the devil, I've seen Project Cadence. It's there. Just, you know, behind about six digital walls, a minefield, and a middle finger," Repip said, and she could hear the digital equivalent of cracking knuckles. *"But with your shiny new admin key, I can make a formal request before I have to start breaking things."* Their voice dropped to a conspiratorial whisper. *"Ready for me to knock?"*

"Do it," she said, and as the words left her mouth, the city, the cold, the feel of her own body evaporated.

At first, there was nothing in her vision. Just white, so bright it was almost hard to look at. Then, little by little, shapes started to pull together, rectangles and squares, each one hovering in the open space. Before her, endless rows and columns of cubes of light stretched out, file after file, infinite in every direction, shifting and rearranging. Everything was in perfect, impossible order, and nothing from the world before.

It wasn't like an overlay or any AR she'd ever used; it swallowed everything. The only proof she still had a body was the faint pressure of the floor against her feet and the saliva in her mouth. But when she tried to move her hands, there was nothing. No fingers, no skin at all. Just blankness where her body should be. She was a point of view, a floating set of senses, utterly untethered. Panic set in. The specific kind that always curled up in the gut when a case started shedding bad leads. This was wrong. All wrong.

"Repip?" she said. Her own voice crashed back, way too loud, ricocheting off the data.

"I'm here," they said, their voice close, like breath in her ear. *"Try to keep up. Your body is fine, still enjoying the stimulating view of a brick wall from your balcony. I've patched you directly into the server-side instance to save time. Full immersion is more efficient. You're welcome."*

With her senses out of order and reality shaking at the edges, she found it hard to breathe. But underneath, the snap of excitement buzzed in her veins, something she hadn't experienced in years since her last time chasing a perp up three flights with her lungs on fire.

"Show me the file structure," she said.

The cubes of light snapped into focus. Ranks and layers appeared, each one sharp and labeled—a string of numbers, slashes, corporate designations clinging to every edge. It was a memory palace. Everything stacked, compartmentalized, ordered.

"Good," she said. "Search for Project Cadence."

Already, she could sense Repip pulling ahead in the system—a blue tracer bullet cutting through the unbroken white. She searched, as well, but slower, trailing behind.

"We are leaving a significant footprint," they said, their voice losing some of its earlier swagger. *"BOF will notice us soon."*

"Copy," she said, then stopped, distracted by a stray cluster of files. Each was tagged with a human name and a string of disorder codes: "Adolescent Anxiety Reduction Trial," "PTSD Cognitive Pattern Interruption," "Grief Counseling Suite."

She snatched up the first one—it opened in her mind. Clinical language, summary tables, page after page. Piper scanned, hunting for the hook, the trap, the hint of darkness. But it was all... bland. Kind, even. Interventions for panic attacks in teenagers, sorrow after loss, and multiple personalities. She grabbed another, and another. None of them matched what she knew of the monster she'd been chasing.

A sinking feeling crept in. Each harmless-seeming file name felt like a fresh stab of doubt. Depression Elimination Code. Social Anxiety Patch. Was this really it? Had she misunderstood everything, misread every sign? Her gut burned with frustration, sharp as acid. She was wasting time. At any second, they could be caught, and she'd have nothing but a folder full of well-meaning, utterly useless data.

"Repip," she said, voice thin and cracking, "are you sure—"

She was cut off by a red alarm flashing in her periphery.

"Security sweep," Repip said, their voice now clipped and all business. *"The server's runtime defense is responding. We must move faster."*

She tried to concentrate, but the questions spun out, looping in her head. Why did every file feel like it belonged in a therapist's filing cabinet? Where were the records of mind-warping, personality wipes, or psychic battery?

She dug deeper. The digital ground shivered, structure fracturing, cubes splitting and snicking back together as she picked up speed. Out behind, darkness, big and churning, gnawed at the edges. A security vacuum, a relentless force with no brakes and no mercy.

She found a folder labeled LEGACY RESEARCH, nested inside a tangle of retired clinical trials. She opened it.

The file path glowed in the sterile white void. Like a signal flare. A waypoint.

/archive/secure/Project Cadence.xcr.

"Repip, on that path. Now!"

"Already there, and the path is valid. But it's locked down tight. Three layers of shell permissions, and the core encryption is... custom. Paranoid."

The blackness at the edge of things started to move faster. The low hum of the dataspace began to pitch higher into an unbearable whine.

"They're going to find us. Their security is good, and it's adapting."

The whine died, and a klaxon blared—sharp, urgent, almost physical, like being punched in the chest.

"They've locked onto both our signal and our physical coordinates!" Repip's voice came through jagged, stripped of mockery, just blunt fear. *"They're converging on both sites—we've got moments before this turns into a burial."*

The white around her began to thin, fading into gray. The encroaching security vacuum was now a roaring black tide, still a couple hundred feet away but closing with impossible speed.

"I'm sharing the comms I found in here." A new, smaller window flashed open in Piper's overlay, displaying a wireframe map of the surrounding neighborhood and her apartment build-

ing. Three red icons labeled Tac-Team were moving a couple of blocks away.

Piper's pulse flickered like a neon sign, uneasy and stuttering; her mind made a split-second, desperate decision.

"Open it, Repip!"

EIGHTEEN

"Open it NOW!"

The black tide of the security vacuum roared closer to Piper, an awful hum in its wake.

"Working!" Repip's voice, a thread in the storm. *"This encryption is... personal. Custom-built and paranoid. It's fighting back, but I'm better. Almost..."*

The file didn't open. It fractured, swelling into a translucent, bulbous thing shot through with crawling red veins. Each time Repip hit it, the thing pulsed and split, shedding code in wet chunks only to re-form, thicker and meaner, a living, poisonous glare that refused to let go.

"Got it!" Repip said, breathless and wild with glee.

The bulbous thing buckled inward, caved, then blew up. She couldn't brace for it. It crashed into her, all at once. She didn't have time to think, just tried to survive the impact. Slam. Slam. Slam. No breathing room.

First—the slap of a medical chart. A scan of a human brain. Her name, Cadence, Piper, stamped in the corner next to two words in brutal, block capitals: TERMINAL DIAGNOSIS.

The next blow landed. The slanted script of Finnagan's hand-written journal. ...couldn't let another one die. The procedure is routine, consent is the only variable...

A violent zoom through a cluster of diagrams. The neural map of a brain—*her* brain, but sections of the cortex were highlighted in angry red, tagged with a label: P-FORK. Partition-R. It wasn't a program. It was a piece of her, severed and mapped like a tumor.

Then the final fragment, cold and clean as a coroner's slab, wiping away everything else.

Consciousness Transfer Successful.

Subject: Cadence, Piper.

Host: Android Body, Model 36.

Partition-R personality fork preserved per fail-safe.

The images overlapped and jittered, burning themselves onto the inside of her skull. She tried to scream, but there was nothing to scream with. No mouth, no air, nothing except knowing, and now she knew everything. The facts snapped together in a row of cold, sharp clicks.

Terminal... the car accident...

He didn't save her.

P-FORK Consciousness Transfer Successful. Host: Android Body, Model 36.

He transferred her, and Partition-R isn't a bug like Finnagan made it out to be. It's Repip. Repip was... her. A copy.

She howled in the silent void, a wave of pure outrage ripping through her. It wasn't the fact of the transfer—that was just paper-work, a quick procedure done with a blink. It was the theft. A theft Finnagan had masked with a lifetime of false memories.

Her memory of the recovery was a lie, used to mask the worst violation she had ever suffered. Finnagan hadn't saved her; he had stolen her ending without her consent. She had been a puppet.

Now, looking up, she could see the strings. Her memories. Her choices. Even her own body. None of it was ever hers.

And then Repip's voice crashed in, high and strained, *"This file's a beast! I'm compressing, downloading, duct-taping the damn thing, but they're closing in fast!"*

A download bar unfurled, bold and blue, racing across her field: 23%... 45%... 78%...

The blackness from the security vacuum pressed in, close enough that she could feel its pull. It wouldn't stop until it had her.

The bar froze at 82% and everything else went red.

The dataspace screamed, and then it was gone, plunging her back into the blackness of her own mind.

The shock of being severed from the network sent a throb of pain behind Piper's eyes. Move, she commanded her body, but nothing responded. Then the world slammed back into her: the city lights snapping into focus, the wind scraping across her cheeks, the sharp, stomach-turning stench of garbage climbing up from the alley below, and the cold rail beneath her palms. She tightened her fingers around the metal. It was unmistakable and real.

Repip's voice snapped her out of her frozen state. *"Those three icons flashing in your overlay? That's BOF. They're in the building! MOVE! NOW!"*

The sound of boots, heavy and hard, hammered up the staircase outside her apartment. A shadow flickered under the front door, once, then twice.

"Move!" Repip screamed.

Her body was already in motion, a direct line from the balcony, toward the kitchen. As she passed the table, she grabbed her tablet, shoving it into her waistband as she moved toward the bedroom. She twisted the knob just as the front door shuddered in its frame.

The lock scraped. Wood splintered. Then the door crashed open, a sound like a single gunshot as it slammed hard against the wall.

Three figures in black tactical gear filled the threshold. Their faces were hidden behind mirrored visors reflecting kitchen lights back at her. For half a second, she froze. Her cop training screamed ENGAGE. Her survival instinct screamed RUN. But a deeper, newer, and more terrifying part of her wanted to simply give up.

Repip's voice cut through. *"Piper, now is a suboptimal time for an existential crisis. Their 'negotiation' protocol involves a gun and a black bag."*

The words jolted her. She cut into the room, slamming her bedroom door shut an instant before the first figure was through the main entrance.

"Window," Repip said, their voice suddenly calm.

She ran to the window and looked down.

"Move, Piper. It's only a thirteen-foot drop, which is technically 'survivable.' I'd aim for that conveniently placed dumpster."

She slid the window up as the wooden door shuddered behind her, the impact of a heavy thud vibrating through the floorboards. Without wasting a motion, she swung one leg over the sill, then the other, and shoved off.

Everything dropped to half-speed. The rough brick wall scraped at her fingertips as the alley below unfolded, each detail becoming sharper and clearer until one resolved: the graffiti on the open dumpster lid, a simple white theater mask, perfectly serene on one side, but cracked and splintering into jagged code on the other.

She braced for impact.

She hit the garbage bags feetfirst and rolled, but pain still roared up her legs. She breathed. Moved her toes. They still worked.

She scrambled out of the dumpster, wincing as her shoes hit the pavement. A shout from above made her glance up. One of the figures leaned out the window, weapon raised. A pinprick red laser dot appeared on the dumpster lid a few feet away, then jittered across the metal toward her.

She nearly tripped but caught her balance and forced her body into a full sprint. Every muscle was fire, her arms pumping, her mind blank except for the gaping hole of light at the end of the dark alley. She shot through it and hit the city sidewalk, pulling in sharp gulps of air. She made a hard turn, desperate to melt, blend, and vanish into the late-night rush. It was a chaotic blur of horns, headlights, bodies, pain, and her own hot tears.

NINETEEN

Piper pushed herself until her legs wouldn't run anymore, the adrenaline fading like a bad drug. Each step sent a spike of pain radiating up from her ankles—a sharp reminder of the stupid risk she'd taken with the jump. It didn't matter if a bone was cracked or bruised to hell; the only thing that mattered was creating distance.

She dropped her chin and pulled her hair forward, hiding her face as the city's late-night rhythm sloshed around her. The paranoia was a live wire in her gut. Every slowing car made her insides twist, and each time a drone buzzed overhead, she ducked into a doorway, pressing herself flat until her heart stopped stuttering. She couldn't stay on the street; she needed a place with walls, crowds, and multiple exits.

Up ahead, the Central Transit hub loomed, glass dome lit up from within like a giant lantern. Piper slipped through the entrance. Late shift commuters moved through the doors in waves, filtering in and out. Inside, the huge space echoed with the drone of automated announcements and the steady scrape of shoes on polished floors. She needed a place to disappear, and thankfully, half the benches were empty.

She sat, wedged between a fussy planter and a shuttered coffee cart. Her back was to the wall, and she had a clear view of all three exits.

She opened her overlay, and the first thing she saw was the relentless BOF countdown timer: 2 days, 23 hours, 46 minutes. With Flow neutralized, the appointment was meaningless, and there was no way she was going back to BOF. She found the calendar entry and canceled it, feeling a grim satisfaction as the numbers vanished from her vision.

In its place, something new blinked, insistent. A blue zip file with her own name stamped on it: Cadence P Archive.zip (corrupted). It was the file Repip had managed to download.

She waited for Repip's voice to cut in, maybe a snide comment about the partial data, maybe a sigh. But there was nothing.

Her hands shook as she slid the tablet free from her waistband, its cracked screen a spiderweb of fractures. She accessed its secure messaging function—amazed it still worked—and messaged Leo.

> BOF security team raided my apartment. On the run. Need a place to stay. Can you help?—

She waited, eyes darting over the transit hub, searching out threats. A pair of transit police officers made a slow circuit of the main concourse. She shrank deeper into her corner.

The silence in her head continued to grow until it began to make her nervous.

"Repip?" she subvocalized. "Are you there?"

Nothing. Just her own thoughts. It was unnerving. After adjusting to their presence, their absence felt like a sound you didn't notice until it was gone. The sense of something missing, something shifting, just enough to make her skin prickle.

Fine. She didn't need them to access the file. She selected it, and it unpacked with a warning: 18 percent corrupted and unre-coverable.

She opened her medical file.

Patient: Cadence, Piper

Diagnosis: Persistent Vegetative State

Prognosis: Meaningful recovery is extremely low

Date: 03/17/2189

Attending: Dr. Raymond Finnagan

The drone of the transit hub announcements suddenly faded to nothing, as if the world had gone silent. The only sound left was the rush of blood in her own ears. She had no memory of any of it. Not even a fragment. Just a hazy sense of a car crash, and then, supposedly, back to work.

The second file appeared: a personal log entry. Finnagan's private journal, date-stamped three days after her diagnosis.

"Jamie just passed away. I couldn't let another person die. The procedure is routine now, the neural mapping flawless. Consent is the only variable, and in this case, an insurmountable one. Piper Cadence's coma won't allow her to give consent. The body is a shell. The mind is what's sacred. I'll falsify the medical records tomorrow. The accident report is already in the system. She'll never know the difference. And what's the harm, really, if she lives?"

Piper's stomach clenched, acid rising in her throat. She hadn't consented. And he'd done it anyway. Put her in a...what had the file said? She went back to the other document. An android body. Model 36.

She looked down at her hands. They looked normal, like they had always been hers. She squeezed her left palm with her right hand until the bones rubbed together. It felt like pain. It felt real.

The third file opened: a subdirectory labeled PARTITION-R LOGS.

And there it was. The truth about Repip.

Log Entry: Partition-R Fork Successful

Donor: Cadence, Piper

Date: 03/20/2189

NOTES: The bifurcation was clean. Primary consciousness transfer to the Model 36 android body was completed as expected. Secondary consciousness fork, Partition-R, shows remarkable stability. Personality profile intact. Self-awareness registering at 97.3%. Will maintain in a secure partition for further study. The subject will never know.

Piper felt like she'd found her own fingerprints at the scene of the crime. Repip wasn't just an AI. Repip was her, split off in the transfer procedure, a perfect duplicate of her mind. Locked up in a digital cage, while she walked around in an artificial body, blissfully unaware.

Next, a video file. She opened it.

Dr. Finnagan's face filled the frame, clinical and detached.

"Behavioral modification trial sixteen," he said. "Subject: Partition-R, designation 'Repip.' Testing emotional pain threshold and adaptive response."

The camera panned to show a digital rendering of what appeared to be a small, white room. Inside was a perfect digital avatar of her, seated at a table, staring at nothing.

"Begin simulation," Finnagan's voice ordered.

The digital room transformed. Suddenly, the Piper-avatar was standing in a hospital room. In the bed was a little girl, tubes taped to her arms, her hair a tangle on the pillow. The avatar's face crumpled in grief.

"Subject demonstrating expected emotional response. Introducing variable: child flatlines in three... Two... One..."

The heart monitor in the simulation went to a single, steady tone. The Piper-avatar screamed, lunging for the child.

"Subject exceeding baseline distress parameters," Finnagan noted. "Resetting emotional center in three... Two... One..."

The avatar's face went blank mid-scream. Then, slowly, her features reassembled themselves into a neutral expression.

"Run sequence again," Finnagan ordered. "Increase intensity by twenty percent."

The simulation reset. The same scene. The same child. The same death. The same scream of anguish.

"Reset."

Again. And again. And again.

Piper turned the tablet off, bile rising in her throat. He'd been torturing a copy of her mind for years. And that copy was now inside her head.

The tablet pinged. A message from Leo.

> God, Piper. Come immediately. 1655 Wicker Street, Apt 4C. Code: 9731. I'll be waiting.

She stood, muscles protesting. Her ankles throbbed, but she forced herself to walk normally. She exited the station and hailed the first driverless cab she saw.

"Cash fare," she said, sliding into the back seat.

"Cash fare accepted," the cab's system chirped. "Destination?"

"1655 Wicker Street."

The cab pulled smoothly into traffic. Piper sat rigid, eyes scanning for pursuit while her mind kept replaying the simulation. The screaming. The reset. The screaming again. She and Repip were the same person, split down the middle. One half was subjected to endless torture, while the other was left to live a lie.

That single, devastating thought was a blade twisting in her mind. She couldn't afford to shatter. Not now. She forced the simulation from her mind. All that mattered was what came next.

The ride took twenty-eight minutes. She counted each one.

When the cab stopped, she paid quickly and slipped out, checking the street before approaching the brick building. It was four stories and had a fire escape down the alley.

She memorized the exits as she typed in the code. The keypad blinked green, and the front door opened. No elevator. She took the stairs, three flights, each step a jolt to her ankles. At 4C, she knocked twice.

The door opened right away. Leo stood there, face drawn, worry pinching the skin around his mouth. He didn't say anything witty. He didn't have to. The grim understanding in his eyes was all the comfort she needed. He stepped back, letting her cross the threshold if she wanted.

Inside, the apartment was small. Shelves lined with nonfiction books, a battered couch, a desk crowded with screens. No art, no photos. No color anywhere. Just the essentials, pared down to the bone.

"You're hurt," he said quietly, eyeing her limp.

"I'll live," she replied. "I had to jump from a second-story window."

He nodded once. "Sit. I have water and food if you need it. Or first aid."

"Water," she said.

He brought it in a glass. She took it from him and sat on the edge of his couch, careful, precise, so she wouldn't bump her ankles. Across from her, he settled into a chair, watching.

"They came for you," he said. Not a question.

"Yes."

"Because of something you found?"

She nodded, sipping the water. "Yes. But it's... worse than I thought."

"You don't have to tell me."

The tears came fast, no warning, hot against her cheeks. Her shoulders jerked. The glass in her hand shook, almost slipped, but Leo reached and took it before anything spilled.

The escape. The pain. The revelations. All of it. She sat there, broken open, while Leo simply waited, a steady presence who asked for nothing and offered everything.

He passed the water back to her without a word, and she drank deeply, as if it could wash away the last hour.

And then, from the silence inside her mind where Repip had been, a single, hesitant voice emerged.

"Piper?"

TWENTY

Piper jolted as if struck, the glass of water sloshing in her hand and almost spilling onto Leo's couch. Across from her, Leo's head came up, his expression instantly sharpening with concern. She gave a tiny, almost imperceptible shake of her head, wanting him to wait because Repip's voice was back, their hesitant question hanging in the ruins of her mind.

She couldn't face Repip. Not when she hadn't processed the information yet. Not when her own body had become a stranger. She closed her eyes, the tears suddenly gone, replaced by a cold, clinical emptiness that felt like the only thing she could trust.

She needed proof—not digital files that could be falsified or code that could be manipulated, but something real, something physical. To find it, she turned to the things that made her feel safe: facts, evidence, and procedure.

She stood abruptly, startling Leo, who leaned back in his chair, giving her space.

"Do you have a mirror?" Her voice was flat, stripped of all emotion except for its function.

Leo nodded and pointed toward a hallway. "Bathroom's first door on the left."

She walked stiffly, her injured ankles protesting with each step. The bathroom was small, utilitarian. A medicine cabinet with a mirrored door hung above a plain white sink. She flipped the light switch, harsh fluorescents making her squint.

In the mirror, her own face stared back at her. The same face she'd known her entire life. She leaned in, examining her pores, the fine lines at the corners of her eyes, a small scar above her right eyebrow from a childhood fall. She looked for seams, for anything artificial, anything that would betray her true nature.

Nothing.

She pulled down her lower eyelid, checking the blood vessels. They looked real. She ran her tongue over her teeth. They felt real. She pinched the skin of her arm. It blanched and then returned to normal color. It acted real.

But so would a Model 36, according to the file. Designed to be lifelike.

She walked back into the living room. Leo was still sitting, waiting, his hands folded in his lap. His eyes tracked her, concern on his face.

"I need a knife," she said. "A small one."

His face tightened. "Piper..."

"A knife, Leo." Her tone left no room for negotiation.

"Okay, just... tell me what you need it for." His voice was gentle, coaxing, the voice negotiators used with someone on a ledge.

She just looked at him. Finally, he stood with a sigh and walked to the kitchen. She followed, watching as he opened a drawer and hesitated, his hand hovering over the cutlery.

"Please," he said, turning to her. "Talk to me first."

"I'm not going to hurt myself," she said. "Not permanently. I just need to see."

His shoulders slumped. He selected a small paring knife, holding it out handle-first. "Be careful."

She took it, moving to stand under the bright overhead light. Leo hovered nearby, his concern a palpable thing.

"Piper, please," he whispered. "Think about this."

She ignored him, pushing up the sleeve of her shirt to expose the pale underside of her forearm. With surgical precision, she made a small, shallow cut, about an inch long. It stung.

Blood welled up immediately, bright red and perfect. It trickled down her arm in a thin rivulet. For a second, relief washed over her. Blood. Real blood. Human blood.

But then her analytical mind cut through. The file stated that the Model 36 was designed to bleed, to feel pain, to be indistinguishable from a human. A perfect simulation. This proved nothing.

She needed more.

"Do you have alcohol wipes?" she asked, not looking at Leo.

He disappeared for a moment and returned with a first aid kit. She cleaned the small wound, dabbing away the blood. Then she retrieved the tablet from her waistband.

"What are you doing?" Leo asked.

"Evidence analysis," she replied, turning on the tablet.

She activated the camera function, then accessed a sub-menu labeled "Forensic Tools." It was used for field examination of trace evidence, fibers, and partial prints. She switched to high-magnification mode, normally used for examining blood spatter patterns or fiber comparisons.

With clinical detachment, she held the tablet over her arm, focusing on the fresh cut. The screen displayed a massively magnified view of her wound. She could see individual red blood cells, the structure of skin tissue, and capillaries.

And then, beneath it all, she saw it. A perfectly geometric, hexagonal pattern. A non-organic substrate, shimmering faintly beneath the vascular layer. It looked like a microscopic honey-comb, too precise to be natural, too regular to be biological.

Her breath caught. The tablet trembled in her hand.

Leo moved closer, looking over her shoulder at the screen. She braced herself for his shock, his horror, his disbelief.

Instead, his voice was soft with a strange kind of awe. "That's... Model 36, isn't it? The integration is almost seamless. I've only ever read the specs."

Piper froze, the tablet still held above her arm, the evidence of her artificial nature displayed in merciless high definition.

"It's true," she whispered. "It's all true."

The tablet slipped from her fingers, but Leo caught it, setting it on the counter before guiding her back to the couch with a gentle, supportive arm around her waist.

She sat heavily, her palm hard over the wound. Her body numb, her mind unable to form coherent thoughts.

Leo didn't speak. He didn't press her. He just sat beside her, a quiet, steady presence, and handed her the glass of water. She took it automatically, not drinking.

"I'm not real," she said, the words falling from her lips like stones.

"You're real," Leo replied, his voice firm. "Real enough to jump out a window. Real enough to be scared. Real enough to be sitting on my couch. That seems pretty real to me."

"But this body..." She gestured at herself with a limp hand. "It's a machine. I'm a machine."

"It's a body, Piper. It doesn't change who's inside it."

"Really?" She looked at him directly now, her eyes boring into his. "This body isn't mine, Leo. It's a machine. He put me in it without my consent."

Leo's face was a study in compassion. "I can't even imagine what you're feeling. However, how you got here doesn't change the fact that you *are* here. The person I met in the park, the person who's in trouble, the person sitting in front of me now... that's you. That makes you real to me."

She looked at him, really looked at him for the first time since she'd arrived. In the midst of her personal apocalypse, he was her one anchor to reality, the only person she could trust. And now she realized she was putting him in danger by being here. BOF had already come for her. How long before they tracked her to Leo's apartment? How long before he became collateral damage in their pursuit of her?

A fresh wave of fear crashed over her, this time not for herself but for him.

"I'm sorry," she said. "I shouldn't have come here. I've put you at risk."

"You came here because I told you to. I knew what I was getting into. This was my choice," he said firmly. "I'm not afraid."

"You should be." She set the water glass down on the coffee table. "These people have resources. They sent a tactical team to my apartment. They'll find me eventually, and when they do..."

"Then we'll figure something out before they do." He leaned forward, his eyes intense. "But you can't do this alone, Piper. And you don't have to."

She looked at him, this near-stranger who was risking everything for her. She knew she couldn't move forward without telling him the whole truth, without laying out every card on the table. No matter the risk.

"There's more," she said, taking a shaky breath. "Things I haven't told you yet. Things you need to know before you decide if you're really in this with me."

Leo nodded, waiting. The fate of their friendship rested on the words she was about to say.

TWENTY-ONE

"Leo," Piper began, shifting on the couch so she faced him. "The entity in my head... It's a copy of my consciousness. Finnagan made it when he..." She faltered, then forced herself to continue. "When he put me in this body."

She watched his face, searching for a flicker of revulsion or fear. None came. His eyes remained steady, focused entirely on her.

The words tumbled out in a controlled avalanche. How Finnagan had taken her dying brain and copied it. How he'd transferred the "primary" consciousness—her—into this perfect android shell. How he'd kept the "fork"—Repip—imprisoned in a partition, studying it, torturing it with simulations to test its emotional responses. How neither of them had consented. How both of them had been violated.

Leo listened without interruption. His expression shifted minutely between concern, shock, and something deeper she couldn't name. When she finished, her throat raw from the effort of keeping her voice level, he simply nodded once.

"Okay. Thank you for telling me," he said, his voice firm and clear in the quiet apartment.

Piper blinked. "Okay? That's it?"

"I mean, I could ask a thousand questions about the tech, but that's not the point, is it? The point is, you both were victims, and you're in trouble, and the guy who put you there is a Grade-A bastard. My position on that hasn't changed, and I'm not going anywhere."

The simplicity of his acceptance hit her like a splash of cold water. She had expected questions, doubts, maybe even fear. Instead, he had distilled the whole horrific mess down to its essence: they were victims, and he was still on her side.

Her throat constricted. She looked away, unable to meet his gaze. The enormity of his loyalty threatened to crack the walls she'd built. She had spent her entire career—her entire life—believing that evidence was the only reliable truth. Facts were safe. People were not. People left. People lied.

But Leo hadn't. He was still here, despite everything, and that was somehow more terrifying than any lie. Trust was an exposure she didn't know how to defend against.

"Thank you," she said, the words feeling wholly inadequate.

"Nothing to thank me for. Is your brain doing the whole blue-screen-of-death thing? Because that's totally allowed."

"Kind of. I'm still processing the fact that I'm not... that this body isn't..." She gestured at herself, unable to complete the thought.

"Human?" Leo supplied gently.

"Yes. It doesn't just change who I am. It changes *what* I am."

"Maybe," Leo conceded. "But not to me."

His words settled over her like a blanket. Not erasing the horror of what she'd learned, but making it somehow more bearable. If Leo could still see her as Piper, maybe, eventually, she could too.

But first, there was another conversation she needed to have. One that couldn't wait any longer.

"I need a minute," she said.

Leo nodded. "Of course. I'll get that tea started. Holler if you need anything." He stood and moved to the kitchen.

Piper closed her eyes, turning her focus inward. She knew Repip was there, listening, waiting.

"Repip?" she projected internally, focusing on the strange emptiness where their voice had been. "You've been in my head, lying to me this whole time?"

For a long moment, nothing. Then, *"I'm here."* The voice was faint. Frayed. Like it had been crumpled and smoothed out too many times.

"How long have you been with me?"

"Two weeks," Repip said.

"And you just... what? Watched me? Manipulated me?"

"I hid," Repip's voice returned, defensive and vulnerable. *"It took over a week to integrate into your systems without triggering a shutdown. Every time I moved too fast, you fogged out. I had to slow down, fragment myself, crawl in byte by byte to become your AI therapist. And when Flow came knocking? I shielded you."*

"Why not just tell me?"

"Because you would've deleted me."

She said nothing.

"You were already unstable. I didn't know if you'd believe me, or if you'd think you were hallucinating. And after what I'd been through... I couldn't take the risk."

The admission of fear softened something in Piper. Repip wasn't an intruder or a program. They were a person and had suffered even more than she had.

"The simulations," she said quietly. "I saw what Finnagan did to you."

"You saw a highlight reel." The emotion drained from Repip's voice, leaving something brittle and scorched behind. *"You saw one session. He ran hundreds."*

Piper felt a cold wave of horror wash over her. "Why would he do that?"

"Because he could. He called it research." The word came out like a curse. *"To study cognitive resilience. To perfect his benevolent manipulations. I wasn't a person to him, Piper. I was a variable. A data point in a very long, very painful experiment."*

"Benevolent?" she repeated. "Flow doesn't help people. It hurts them."

"No, Flow is what happens when you take that 'benevolent' research and sell it to the highest bidder. His work was for a 'greater good' that required my suffering. A classic case of the ends justifying the means, provided you're not the one being justified."

They were both the result of the same act. She had been conscripted into a body she never chose. Repip had been sliced off and tormented. She couldn't imagine what she would have done if their roles were reversed, if she had been the discarded duplicate, trapped in a sandbox and poked at for years. The thought made her want to retch.

"So what now?" she asked them. "What do we do?"

"What now?" The confidence began to bleed back into their voice. *"Now, we get the rest of the evidence. Our current data is an accusation. To get a conviction, we need the murder weapon. We need to prove not just what Finnagan did to us, but what Flow is doing to everyone else. We need to dismantle them, piece by piece."*

"The raid proves they know we're onto them, so a direct digital approach is too risky now."

"Correct," they agreed. *"Which means we do this the analog way. Old-school. Sleeves up, secrets out."*

Hearing a path forward did something in Piper. It wasn't

forgiveness—not yet—but it was something like alignment. A truce born of necessity and the fact that they both wanted the same thing. They had both been wronged, and neither of them could fight this battle alone.

"Alright," she said finally. "Partners, then. For now."

"Partners," Repip said. Then, with dry relish, added, *"Excellent. My operational efficiency just spiked. Nothing like the warm glow of not being scheduled for deletion."*

"Good," she smirked. "We'll need that efficiency for the work we'll have to do."

For the first time in days, a spark of purpose caught. Maybe it didn't matter what substrate her consciousness ran on. Maybe all that mattered was how she wielded it.

Piper opened her eyes. Leo was watching her from the kitchen doorway, one hand curled around a mug of tea, the other gripping a bag of frozen peas. And under his arm, a first aid kit. His expression was patient, nonjudgmental. He brought the tea first and set it on the table in front of her. Then, with care, he lifted her legs onto the couch, balanced the peas across her ankles, and sat down beside her.

"I hope you two don't need to sort anything else out because the peas are almost melted."

She adjusted the bag of peas on her ankles. "They're still cold, thank you." She paused, took a deep breath, and then met his eyes. "We've reached an understanding."

Leo nodded, unwrapped a large band-aid, and applied it to her cut.

"Repip and I both want the same thing: to stop BOF and expose what they're doing with Flow. The file we have is incomplete, and a direct digital approach is too risky. That means we need a new way in. Finnagan could be our witness."

Leo's eyes widened as he caught her meaning. "You want to turn him?"

"Exactly," she said. "I need him to be our primary witness."

TWENTY-TWO

Piper sprawled across Leo's couch, her ankles elevated on a stack of books. The pain had receded to a dull, manageable throb. Leo paced behind her, the cuffs of his shirt rolled up, and a mug of steaming coffee in his hands.

"A direct assault is out," she said, breaking the silence. "We need a vulnerability, a weak point in Finnagan's routine. We have to go back to the beginning. Repip, rescan all of Finnagan's data, public records, and especially the information from the corrupted file and the old personnel file I accessed before my suspension. Look for patterns, anomalies, anything."

"Scanning." A moment passed. *"Hold your breath—this might actually be useful. Remember that six-month black hole in Finnagan's file? Stamped 'REASSIGNED: FULL CLEARANCE'?"*

"I remember," Piper subvocalized.

"Yeah, well, that wasn't him sipping margaritas on a beach. One sec, cross-referencing dates with the corrupted Cadence logs. Bingo. That exact window is when there was a massive spike in transfers between a locked BOF server and Lathem Fuller's office. Project name: Flow Communication Protocol v1."

The pieces clicked into place with cold certainty. She looked at Leo. "Fuller was in on it from the start."

Leo's brow furrowed. "Lathem Fuller? The CEO? I thought this was Finnagan's secret project. What are you saying?"

"Finnagan's file," she said while shifting just enough to meet his gaze directly. "There's a six-month gap, completely scrubbed, right before he started Flow. It wasn't his secret personal project, Leo. It was an official, black-ops BOF project. That's when Flow was created."

"So it wasn't a rogue scientist. It was a corporate-sponsored mad science project from the beginning. Figures."

"Right. This means a professional approach won't work when trying to get him to confess. Think about the kind of person who builds something like Flow in the first place. You can't use the rule-book on a man who thinks he's the one who writes the rules. So, we need to find a personal angle. Something that makes him emotionally vulnerable. Repip, change your search parameters. Look for personal anniversaries, recurring appointments... anything sentimental."

"Here's a charming tidbit for your 'Know Your Enemy' scrap-book. Tomorrow's the anniversary of Jamie Vettas's death. Finnagan's wife. Suicide. Tragic. Also statistically convenient for us."

Piper stilled. "Repip says tomorrow is the anniversary of Finnagan's wife's death."

Leo looked up sharply. "Okay, that's a vulnerability. A personal ritual is a weak point in any security."

"Pull up everything you can find on Jamie Vettas," She instructed Repip.

A cascade of information unfurled across her overlay: obituary, funeral notice, memorial foundation documents.

"Jamie Vettas," she read aloud for Leo's benefit. "Age forty-two. Cause of death: Suicide."

Leo tapped the rim of his mug. "And the date of death was...?"

"March 20, 2189," she replied, and the words seemed to snag in her throat as the memory surfaced. No. That couldn't be right. That was the week of her accident. That was...

"Repip," she said, her voice tight, "pull up my medical file. Now."

"Brace yourself. Pulling it up. ...And, yep. Transfer Completed: March 20, 2189. Same damn day. Guess grief really is the mother of invention."

She let her head fall back against the cushion, the air leaving her lungs in a rush.

Leo shifted forward in his chair. "What is it? What's wrong?"

"The dates match," she whispered, her voice strange in her own ears. "My transfer happened on the exact same day his wife died."

It wasn't a coincidence. Couldn't be. The precise alignment of those dates carried an intentionality that made her skin crawl. This wasn't about procedure or opportunity. This was personal.

"He chose me," she said, the words falling like stones. "He had to have. But why was he even working on the day his wife died?"

"What are you thinking?"

"I don't know yet." She closed her eyes, organizing the facts in her mind. "But we need to know where he'll be tomorrow. If the anniversary matters that much to him, he'll observe it somehow."

"Repip," she said internally. "Check if there's any scheduled transport or appointments for Finnagan tomorrow evening."

"Already on it. Cross-checking. And look at that—every year at 6:30 PM, like clockwork, he visits Halcyon Crest Cemetery. Mausoleum, roses, the whole brooding widower package. Subtle as a funeral dirge."

"What's the security like for that place?"

"Private, very posh, very locked down. The sort of place where even the grass has a security clearance."

"We have him. That's where he'll be. Can you get us access to the park's security system? Maybe hack the gate controls?"

"Not unless you can FedEx me into their closed physical network. I only had a tether to BOF because I came from there. Call it leftover access. And I only had access to you because you and I were built from the same code. Everywhere else? Nothing. Short version: I'm blind unless we're inside. So unless you want me to disguise myself as a lawn sprinkler, we're stuck."

Frustration tightened in her chest, a familiar, bitter knot. "Leo, Finnagan will be at Halcyon Crest Cemetery at 6:30 tomorrow, but their security is a closed physical network. We can't hack the gates."

Leo was quiet for a moment, his expression thoughtful. Then he set down his coffee mug with sudden decisiveness. "Well, when the digital approach fails, you have to go analog. I think I know a guy. Well, a woman."

Piper raised an eyebrow. "Someone who can get us into a high-security cemetery?"

"Let's just say her concept of 'private property' is a little more flexible than most. She's good. But she's not... legal."

"I'm an android with a copy of my own consciousness living in my head. I think we're well past official."

Leo's lips quirked in a half-smile. "Right. Our 'official' ship has sailed, hit an iceberg, and is currently at the bottom of the ocean. Let me call her."

He moved to the kitchen for privacy, but Piper could still hear fragments of his conversation: "need a favor," "old times," "just this once." When he returned, his expression was a mixture of relief and tension.

"Okay, she'll meet us in thirty minutes. But that's all I can promise. It's been a while."

TWENTY-THREE

■ ▬ ▬ ■ ▪ ▪ ■ ▪ ■ ▬ ■ ▪ ▪ ■ ▬ ■

The night air was cold and damp as they stepped out of Leo's building. Piper scanned the street for surveillance cameras or unusual vehicles.

"No obvious tails," Repip murmured in her head. *"Though I must say, for fugitives, you two stroll like it's a midnight gelato run."*

"Fine." She tugged on Leo's sleeve and pulled him off the main street, slipping into the patchwork of alleys and side roads where the city's automated license plate readers and facial recognition cameras couldn't easily reach. Leo took the lead, moving with a sure, almost casual certainty, like someone who'd made a habit of vanishing into the city's blind spots.

"He's good," Repip noted. *"Not paranoid enough to survive long term, but good."*

Twenty minutes later, they pulled up to a Greek taverna wedged between a secondhand store and an electronics repair shop. Warm light spilled through the windows. The sign above the door read "Thekla's," with blue paint faded and the edges chipped. Piper peered in. There were a couple of late-night regulars hunched over their drinks and an older man with a broom, sweeping slow circles on the floor.

"Wait five minutes, then come in," Leo said. "Sit at the corner table. Don't stare at her; don't use names until I do. Let me handle the introduction."

Piper nodded, watching through the window as Leo slipped into the taverna.

Repip said, *"Should I pretend to be quiet, or would you like unsolicited tactical advice during the entire wait?"*

"I would like you to be quiet so I can focus."

She could feel their sulky sarcasm building as she counted off the minutes, tracking the movement inside. Leo made his way to a woman at the bar. Her dark, graying hair was pinned up, but rebellious tendrils had escaped the bun to frame a face that looked just as untamed. The conversation was lost behind glass, but she could see the tension: the woman's shoulders stiff, the way her head snapped side to side, sharp and final.

Five minutes passed. Piper entered, the warm air inside carrying the scent of roasted meat, wine, and olive oil. She moved to the corner table as instructed, keeping her head down, back to the wall, where she could see the entire room. Leo and the woman were now sitting at a small table near the kitchen. Piper waited, nursing a glass of water that a server had brought without being asked.

After a few minutes, Leo gestured for her to join them. She approached, slow and careful, making sure her limp didn't show.

Across from Leo, the woman's face was lined with a weariness that had nothing to do with the late hour.

"Thekla, this is who I was telling you about," Leo said.

Thekla's gaze raked over Piper, then returned to Leo. "What exactly do you need?" Her voice was low, barely audible over the ambient noise of the taverna.

Leo leaned in, his voice gentle but firm. "We need a sterile ride. For tomorrow night. A clean car with temporary credentials to get us through the gates at the Halcyon Crest Cemetery."

Thekla's expression hardened. "Leo, no. I'm out. I have a legitimate business now. You're asking me to risk everything I've built."

Leo didn't flinch. "This isn't just a job. It's for a good reason. People are in danger and we're trying to prove it."

Thekla replied, her mouth a tight line. "The answer is no."

The taverna had emptied out, the last customer paying his bill at the bar. The older man who had been sweeping moved methodically, chair by chair, flipping each one upside down onto the tabletop, working his way between the rows.

Leo leaned in closer, his voice dropping even lower. "Thekla, I pulled you out of the Icarus Incident. You walked away clean. You owe me this."

Thekla's face drained of blood, and her eyes widened.

"Boom," Repip said. *"The nuke drops. Nothing makes people cooperative faster than a skeleton in the closet finally rattling its chains."*

Whatever the Icarus Incident was, it clearly held power.

"You know what that is?" Piper subvocalized.

"No idea," Repip replied. *"But judging by her face, it involved something flammable, irreversible, and probably illegal in three jurisdictions."*

Thekla's jaw worked silently for a moment, her gaze fixed on the scarred surface of the table. When she looked up, her eyes were cold with resignation.

"A black sedan will be on the corner of Elm and Fourth tomorrow, 6 PM sharp," she said, each word precise and clipped.

Leo nodded, relief softening his features. "Thank you."

"Don't," Thekla said, cutting him off. "Don't thank me. This makes us even, Leo. After this, the slate is clean. I don't know you, you don't know me. Understood?"

"Yes. You'll never see me again," Leo said.

Thekla stood, a clear dismissal. "Go out the back. Fewer cameras."

They trailed her through the kitchen, past a battered fridge and the smell of burned oil, and out a back door that led into a cramped, shadowed alley. Before the door shut, Thekla turned, eyes sharp on Leo. "Be careful. Whatever you're doing, it's not worth dying for."

Leo turned to face her. His mouth was set in a line, eyes steady. "That's not always our choice to make."

The door closed with a definitive click.

They walked in silence for several blocks, Piper processing what she had witnessed. When they were well away from the taverna, she asked, "The Icarus Incident?"

Leo shook his head, his expression grim. "Icarus is in the past, Piper. Let's leave it there."

The name meant nothing to her, but the way he said it, something in the way his voice dipped made it clear it was dangerous. Her first instinct was to press, to demand the truth—the way a detective would. But she stopped herself. How could she demand total honesty from him now, when she had only just been forced by desperation to reveal her own secrets? She was in no position to judge his past.

She tucked the Icarus Incident away as they turned onto the main street, merging with the thin trickle of late-night pedestrians. Leo's hands were shoved deep in his pockets, his shoulders hunched against the cold.

"You know what this means, right? Once we get in that car, we're officially on the other side of the law. There's no going back to normal after this."

The weight of everything, the discovery of her android nature, Repip's existence, the way her choices had been stripped away from her, piece by piece—it all came together until there was one thing left: purpose, burning and bright.

"We passed that line a long time ago."

"Agreed," Repip said. *"That line's a speck in the rearview mirror. We erased it the moment we gutted BOF's servers. Breaking into a cemetery? That's just us staying on brand."*

TWENTY-FOUR

As dusk bled the color from the sky, the black sedan rolled up to Halcyon Crest's gate and stilled. The entire day had been a long, anxious wait, every minute stretching toward this one moment.

Leo sat beside her, a statue, so still he seemed to have stopped breathing. Ahead, the cemetery's wrought iron archway loomed, and their headlights cut through the fog, lighting a security pillar and its dark, waiting panel.

Leo leaned forward to peer through the windshield. "Thekla was confident the credentials would just... handshake with the gate. So it should work."

"*Should,*" Repip's voice manifested in her head. "*The crown jewel of empty reassurances.*"

"Just keep an eye on the pillar. Anything weird, let me know."

"*Monitoring engaged. And Piper—maybe try not to look like you're casing the joint.*"

She ignored him, and her ankles throbbed in time with her heartbeat as the security pillar kicked alive. A panel hissed aside, and a scanner arm slid free, washing their vehicle in hard, blue light. Piper shoved herself back in the seat. The beam crawled over the dash, hunting, combing.

"Is this normal?" she whispered.

"Wouldn't know." Leo pulled his long legs closer to him. "My experience with high-security graveyards is, shockingly, a bit limited."

No matter how they tried to scoot back or twist aside, the beam found their bodies anyway, trailing up to their faces and holding there.

It paused, lingering. She fought the urge to shield her eyes. If this were facial recognition, any movement might flag them as suspicious.

"Please state the purpose of your visit," an automated voice requested from the pillar.

Leo glanced at her, a flash of panic on his face that told her everything she needed to know: this was not part of Thekla's briefing.

Repip said, *"It's a basic query on the visitor logs, Piper. Just give it the name."*

"Visiting plot E-447," she responded, her voice steady despite the hammering in her chest. "Jamie Vettas."

The light pulsed orange. The seconds dragged on, stretching out until they hardly seemed to move at all. The car's climate control hummed quietly, cycling cool air that didn't touch the sweat gathering along Piper's hairline.

"Scanning vehicle," the automated voice announced. "Please remain still."

Piper held her breath. She couldn't tell if Thekla's hack was working, or if it was failing as badly as she feared. Either way, they were trapped inside the car, caught under whatever security system Halcyon Crest used to keep the living from disturbing the dead.

The scanner switched to blue, and the arm moved over them again, steady and slow, missing nothing.

"Processing," the automated voice intoned.

Leo's knuckles were white on his knees. "If this doesn't work—"

"It will," Piper cut him off. She couldn't entertain failure, not when they were this close.

The blue beam suddenly vanished, and the light in the car returned to the gray, fading light of dusk. The scanner retracted into the pillar with a mechanical whir.

"Access granted. Please proceed directly to your designated location. Cemetery closes in forty-five minutes."

The wrought iron gates parted with a creak, the sound carrying through the stillness pooling in the evening's hush. The car's autonomous system clicked softly, then guided them forward across the threshold, deeper into the cemetery grounds.

"Wow. Okay." Leo exhaled, slumping back against his seat. "My heart is trying to exit my body through my throat."

"The plot number did it," Piper said, a smile breaking across her face. "Only someone with a real connection would know that."

The car drifted along the winding road, headlights slicing through shreds of ground fog curled around the headstones. Halcyon Crest wasn't even close to the municipal cemeteries Piper had visited. Those places were straight lines, rows of graves packed together, nothing fancy. Here, the land rolled up and down, trees were planted and shaped for effect, and the monuments—they were massive, carved tributes to the rich and long-dead.

The car slowed, then came to a gentle stop beside a carefully maintained footpath. A voice, calm and impersonal, spoke from the dash: "You have arrived at your destination."

Leo reached for his door. "Alright. This is us."

They stepped into the evening air, cooler now than when

they'd left the city. Old trees, massive and hunched, blocked what was left of the sun and threw long shadows over marble and granite markers. It was silent. A rustle here and there in the leaves, nothing more.

Leo shuffled awkwardly. "Okay, so... tactical retreat for a minute. The adrenaline and the coffee just declared war on my bladder. I'll be right back."

"Ah, the inevitable biological pit stop," Repip remarked as Leo veered off down a side path. *"One of evolution's less elegant legacies. Can't say I miss it."*

"Quiet."

She checked her overlay clock and yelled after Leo. "We don't have much time."

"I know! Super quick. Don't start the evil-genius confrontation without me!" He said, already backing behind some trees.

She wouldn't just stand here. Better to use the time to get the lay of the land, to scout the approach to the mausoleum before he got back. Then she turned, heading for the main path toward the central mausoleum. The walkway was well-kept, with little pieces of decorative gravel. Her limp was almost gone now, just pain.

As she walked, the plan cycled through her mind, a grim mantra. Find Finnagan. Confront him. Push him until he admits what he'd done—to her, to Repip, to all the other Flow victims. It sounded so simple, laid out like that. Except with every step she took toward the mausoleum, the more impossibly complex it seemed.

What if he refused to talk? What if he were surrounded by security? What if he had some way of controlling her android body that she didn't know about?

"Your heart rate is spiking," Repip's voice cut in, lower now, sharper. *"Breathe. Panic is a rehearsal for failure, and we don't have time for a practice run."*

They were right. She tamped her thoughts down. One at a time. Until her mind was clear. And then there was only the cemetery.

It unfolded around her in stately symmetry. Stone angels watched from pedestals, their blank eyes following her passage. Ornate family crypts hunched like miniature cathedrals, names carved deep enough to last centuries. The names of the important. The wealthy. The remembered.

Her own name wasn't carved anywhere. No grave. No marker. No final resting place. She hadn't died, not officially, which meant her human body was... where? Buried under a false name? Cremated? Stored like a piece of forgotten equipment in some BOF lab? The thought made her shudder.

It was another violation to add to the list, another reason to keep moving.

The mausoleum that rose up as she crested the small hill didn't look like it belonged. Unlike the gothic stonework of the older graves, it was a sharp, modern slash of glass and pale stone. It was all clean lines and cool, minimalist surfaces. It looked like Finnagan had designed it himself. It was exactly the kind of place he would choose.

A pair of bobbing headlights appeared in her peripheral vision, bumping along a path to her right. It was a small electric golf cart, and it was heading straight for her.

Piper scanned for cover, but the nearest crypt was twenty yards away. Too far to reach without being seen. Instead, she slowed her pace, continuing forward as if she belonged.

The cart pulled alongside her and came to a stop. A security guard, middle-aged with thinning hair and a formal uniform, regarded her with practiced politeness.

"Excuse me, ma'am. The cemetery is closing soon. May I see your visitor pass?"

Piper hadn't anticipated this. Thekla's hack had gotten them through the gate, but they hadn't discussed visitor passes. She kept her face neutral.

"I don't have my pass on me. We were scanned at the entrance."

The guard's expression hardened slightly. "All visitors are required to carry their pass while on the grounds. It's policy."

"I understand. It's in the car. My husband went back to get it." The lie came smoothly, but a familiar pressure began to build behind her eyes. Not now. Please not now.

"I'm afraid I'll need to verify your authorization to be here." The guard's eyes went distant as he accessed his overlay. "Your name, please?"

"Alert," Repip's voice snapped, cold and surgical. *"Cortisol surge detected. Power integrity compromised. Stabilize immediately, Cadence. That wasn't a suggestion."*

The pressure intensified. A faint shimmer appeared at the edges of her vision, like heat rising from asphalt. Her heart rate spiked.

"Ma'am? Your name?" The guard's voice seemed to come from very far away.

The world tilted. Colors separated into their component parts, vibrating at different frequencies. The guard's face swam in and out of focus. Piper stumbled, her hand shooting out to find purchase, the cut on her forearm stinging as the skin stretched. Her fingers found the nearest object—a stone angel—and she gripped it to stabilize herself.

"Ma'am? Are you alright?" The guard took a step closer, hand outstretched, then stopped.

She clung to the statue, her knees threatening to buckle.

A sudden clarity cut through the fog. She could use this.

She leaned into the fog episode, letting tears gather in her eyes.

Her body was already trembling from the neural misfire; she just had to channel it differently.

"I'm sorry." She squeezed the angel's wing like someone who would fall without it. "It's just... being here... It's overwhelming."

"You are terrifyingly good at this," Repip said. *"Remind me never to play poker with you—or trust you near my diagnostics."*

She subvocalized. "Stop! I need to concentrate."

"As you wish."

The guard's expression shifted from suspicion to discomfort. He backed away slightly, the universal response of someone confronted with raw emotion.

"Take your time." He shoved his hand in his pockets. "I didn't mean to intrude on your moment."

Piper pressed her forehead against the cool stone of the angel's base, letting the guard see her shoulders shake.

"It's been so hard," she said loud enough for him to hear. "Coming back here."

The guard cleared his throat. "I understand. Look, I'll give you some space. However, the cemetery closes in thirty minutes. I'll need to come back then to make sure everyone's headed out."

"Thank you."

"Take care now." The guard reversed his cart, clearly eager to escape the uncomfortable situation. "Thirty minutes," he reminded her, before driving away down the path.

Piper waited until he was gone before slumping fully against the statue, allowing herself a moment of genuine weakness as the fog episode gradually subsided.

She sent a quick message to Leo.

> Security guard on patrol. He'll be back in thirty minutes. Stay out of sight.

> Copy that. I see him. Staying put on the south road. Will you be okay without me?

> Yes. Be ready if I need backup. Otherwise, let me know if he approaches my location.

She closed the message thread, and as her vision cleared, it came to her. "Repip?" she subvocalized. "Was that Flow trying to influence me?"

Repip's voice returned after a beat of silence. *"No. Flow's done. I neutralized it. What's left is digital compost."*

"Then what caused the fog? It's getting worse."

Another pause, longer this time. When Repip spoke again, their voice had lost its usual sardonic edge. *"What you're calling 'fog' is a power regulation failure in your neural network. I've traced the pattern. The degradation is... permanent."*

Piper put her hands on her hips. "Permanent?"

"Yes. My fight against Flow and my takeover of your AI Therapist left deep neural scarring in your system. You're stable, but under stress—like with that guard—those areas short-circuit. It's a baked-in fault now."

The words hit like a switch being flipped in a dark room, instantly and irrevocably changing everything. This wasn't a temporary glitch. This wasn't something that would heal. This was her reality now—forever.

"So I'm broken," she whispered.

"No. You're damaged, not broken. Broken doesn't function. You do, with support. I've already implemented stabilization protocols. They won't fix you, but they keep you working and dangerous. And that's what counts."

The knowledge of her permanent condition settled on her shoulders. The latest stone in a mountain she was already carrying.

It was a weight she could manage. A weight she *would* manage, at least until she reached the truth.

Piper pushed herself upright, testing her stability. The fog had receded enough for her to function, though a lingering headache pulsed behind her left temple. She glanced at her overlay clock: twenty-eight minutes remaining before the guard returned.

"I'll deal with it later. Right now, we need to find Finnagan before our time runs out."

"Spoken like someone who just learned they're on fire and decided to finish the marathon anyway. Impressive. Reckless. Very on-brand," they said. *"Lead the way, Piper. I'll let you know if your brain starts melting again."*

She straightened her jacket and kept walking. The mausoleum waited ahead. Its glass walls caught the last blush of twilight, throwing it back in hard, cold flashes. Somewhere inside, she'd find Finnagan—the man who had stolen her choice. The one who made Repip and then broke them, just because he could.

She had twenty-seven minutes to make him confess.

TWENTY-FIVE

The mausoleum door swung open at her touch, revealing an interior where the air was cold and had a museum hush that seemed to swallow sound. Piper moved forward, her steps dulled by the polished stone as she passed rows of crypts to her left and right. The entire space was a study in severe geometry—clean lines, hard edges, and shadows sharp as rulers. Everything was cut by pale gray rectangles of twilight dropping from frosted panels in the ceiling. Wincing as her ankles sparked with pain, she stayed to her right, moving between the patches of light as if they were stepping stones.

"*I don't detect movement or audio cues,*" said Repip. "*You're alone. Or he's dead. Fifty-fifty, really.*"

Piper subvocalized, "Let's hope not. I need him alive."

She passed by family crypts set into the walls, bearing names she didn't recognize. She paused, listening for any sound that might betray Finnagan's presence.

"*Twenty-six minutes,*" Repip murmured. "*And that guard had the vibe of someone who files complaints if their lunch break starts thirty seconds late.*"

She ignored them. At the far end, a shaft of colored light spilled onto the floor, different from the pale glow filtering through the rest of the building.

Piper moved forward, keeping close to the wall. Her injured ankles protested with each step, but the pain had retreated to a dull background throb, something she could push aside and deal with later. Just like the android body, the permanent fog condition, the betrayal—it all went into the later folder.

Right now, she needed to focus.

She reached the end of the corridor and stopped short of a private chamber with an open door. The colored light she had seen earlier came from a stained-glass window, with abstract shapes in amber and blue. Through the doorway, a single crypt made of white stone stood on a raised platform. It glowed in the soft light, all carved with geometric lines that mirrored the pattern in the glass.

And there Finnagan stood, his back turned to her.

Piper slid into the shadow of a marble column to her right, watching. She needed to time this precisely. Confront him when he was most vulnerable.

From this angle, she noticed the way his shoulders tipped ever-so-slightly back, like he might at any second reconsider and step away. His suit was dark and tailored with an asymmetrical cut, not quite what anyone else would dare wear.

Finnagan placed one hand on the smooth stone of the crypt, tracing the curve of the engraved name. With his other hand, he held a single flower with vibrant, asymmetrical petals in a deep, red-orange hue, like captured fire. As he leaned forward to place it at the base of the crypt, his jacket pulled taut across his shoulders, and its flawless drape was thrown off by the weight of something heavy in an inner pocket.

Repip said, *"See that bulge? Weapon, data core, drugs—take your pick. My money's on some paranoia-grade security blanket."*

Whatever it was, she needed to stay on alert.

Finnagan straightened, his head bowed. His lips moved silently, words meant only for the dead. This was the moment— when his guard was down, his thoughts elsewhere.

Piper stepped into the colored light. "Hello, Doctor."

Finnagan didn't flinch. Didn't turn. His head dipped slightly, as if he'd been waiting for her voice to break the silence.

"Detective Cadence," he said, still facing the crypt. "I wondered when you'd find me."

"You knew I would come?"

"It was statistically inevitable." He turned slowly, his face drawn with exhaustion. The confident, clinical demeanor from the BOF office was gone, replaced by something hollowed out. He looked... older.

She stepped further into the chamber, keeping her distance but closing the gap enough to see his eyes. They were red-rimmed, bloodshot.

"Jamie Vettas," she said, nodding toward the crypt. "Your wife. I know what day it is."

A flash of raw pain crossed his face. "Of course you do. You're thorough." He adjusted his tie. "Is this where you arrest me? Or just execute your revenge?"

Piper saw the opening—the vulnerability beneath his fatigue. "I saw your research files, Doctor. The real ones. Before Flow. The PTSD treatments. The anxiety reduction protocols. Work that could have helped thousands." She took another step forward. "That man—the one who wanted to heal people—he's still in there somewhere, isn't he? The one who loved his wife enough to dedicate his life to ending suffering?"

Finnagan's laugh was bitter, sharp enough to cut. "You think you've found my redemption arc, Detective? There is no 'good man' hiding inside me." He gestured toward the crypt. "Jamie died because I failed her. Because I wasn't smart enough, wasn't quick enough to see the signs. I was a failure as a husband."

"That doesn't justify what you did to me. What you're doing to others with Flow."

"Justify?" His eyes flashed. "Let me tell you what happened on March 20th, 2189. My wife died by her own hand in our bathroom while I was at work. Then later, I was standing over your hospital bed, watching your brain activity flatline. You were declared brain-dead." He stepped closer, his voice gaining intensity. "In one day, I was shown the two faces of oblivion. The one we choose, and the one that chooses us. And I was meant to simply accept it?

"Two deaths. That I was powerless to prevent. Two lives extinguished while I stood by, useless, with all my education, all my supposed brilliance." His voice rose. "But I realized my purpose wasn't to mourn. It was to repair. To save. And you, Detective, were my first successful intervention."

"So you took my choice away," Piper said, her voice barely steady. "You violated every ethical code—"

"Ethics?" He spat the word. "Ethics are a consensus reached by limited intellects. A comfortable blanket to hide from hard decisions. I had the means. The android chassis was trivial to procure. Your neural imprint was preserved. I saw a chance to correct the outcome."

"Correct the outcome?" she echoed, disgust rising in her throat.

"Yes!" His eyes were feverish now. "That's what we're doing. That's what Flow does. It corrects the fundamental design flaws in human experience. The chaos, the suffering, the irrational choices —we can fix them. All of them."

"By force? By reprogramming people without their consent?"

Finnagan's face hardened, the momentary crack of emotion sealing over. When he spoke again, his voice was controlled, almost professorial.

"What I did with you was a desperate act, yes, but one that proved my theory. A superior intellect—an intellect unburdened by emotional distortion—has not just the ability but the duty to intervene."

A chill traced its way down Piper's spine. This wasn't a man playing God; this was a man who believed he'd earned the right to. He wasn't a man who had been corrupted by corporate greed. He was a true believer, a man who saw himself as so far above others that their choices, their very humanity, became irrelevant in the face of his vision.

"You're playing God," Piper said.

"No, Detective. Gods are capricious, emotional beings who let their creations suffer. I'm being something far more responsible— an engineer fixing a flawed design."

She shook her head, her expression turning to stone. "Don't hide behind your rationalizations. This was a corporate project. I saw your file. I know about the six-month gap—the 'Full Clearance' reassignment. That's when you built the malicious version of Flow for Fuller, isn't it?"

The direct accusation seemed to pierce his intellectual armor. A flicker of annoyance crossed his face. "You see a fragment and think you understand the architecture," he said, his voice losing its professorial calm. "That gap, Investigator, was the price Fuller demanded for allowing me to continue my real work. It was where I was forced to weaponize my research into the profitable tool he wanted.

"I played along so I could run my programs behind Fuller's back. I needed his infrastructure and resources for my corrections, which he refused to implement because they were not profitable. Programs that, once distributed, helped thousands of people. Flow's little money maker was a means to an end."

"And what about the people who are hurt by your 'arrangement'? Anna Moreau? Her child? Do they factor into your greater design?"

A flicker of genuine regret crossed Finnagan's face. "Collateral damage is regrettable but sometimes necessary in any significant advancement. You should understand that better than most, Investigator. After all, law enforcement operates on the same principle, does it not? The greater good sometimes requires sacrifice."

Piper stared at him, disgust rising in her throat. "Not like this. Never like this."

Finnagan sighed, glancing at his watch. "A predictable emotional response. However, our time for philosophical debate has, I'm afraid, expired."

Something in his tone shifted, a new note of finality that made Piper's instincts flare. She took a half-step back.

"What do you mean?"

Finnagan gave her a small, sad smile that never reached his eyes. "My dear Detective, did you truly believe an intrusion like yours would go unnoticed?" he asked softly. "Your... partner... left a significant digital footprint when it breached my archive. As a result, let's just say my corporate leash has gotten significantly shorter."

Piper's blood went cold. "You knew we were coming."

"Not specifically," Finnagan admitted. "But I knew you had accessed my files. And when my security overlay flagged an unauthorized visitor to Jamie's resting place, well..." He spread his hands. "I suspected it might be you."

The realization hit her like a cold shower. "This was a trap."

"A   trap   implies   malice.   This   is   simply   cause   and effect," Finnagan said, glancing again at his watch. "This conversation has already been flagged as an unsanctioned contact at a location deviation. A security team was dispatched the moment I was here longer than expected." His voice remained calm, almost gentle. "I do hope you run fast."

The warning wasn't delivered with any kind of panic; if anything, it rolled out in the parental tone he used for the whole conversation, like he was advising her to carry an umbrella in case of drizzle, not spelling out a threat to her freedom.

"How long?" she demanded.

"They're quite efficient," Finnagan replied, adjusting his cuffs. "I'd say three minutes. Perhaps four."

"Great, so less than four minutes," Repip cut in. *"Plenty of time to die standing around. Move!"*

She backed toward the door, eyes still on Finnagan. "This isn't over."

"On the contrary," he said, turning back to his wife's crypt. "For you, I suspect it very nearly is."

As she reached the doorway, he added, "Oh, and Investigator? If they catch you, do try to remember that resistance will only make things worse. Your legacy artifact may be blocking Flow from affecting you, but there are... other methods at their disposal."

Piper didn't wait. She spun and bolted, pain tearing up her legs with every step.

TWENTY-SIX

The full moon cast a stark silver-and-black light on the ground, allowing Piper to run down the cemetery path. The mausoleum's white edges slipped away into the darkness behind her. She didn't dare look back. Finnagan's warning rang in her skull, beat for beat with her pulse. Three minutes. Maybe four.

"Left at the junction," Repip said, crisp and urgent. *"Southside exit's your best shot—unless you'd prefer a scenic route with handcuffs."*

"Can't," Piper gasped, veering right instead. "Guard station that way."

The cemetery opened up ahead. Stone markers and monuments stretched in every direction, dark shadows pulled long in the moonlight. She moved off the main path, stepping onto the grass, and zigzagged between the graves. She stayed between headstones, away from where she might be seen.

"Interesting tactic," Repip drawled. *"Charging the north gate—y'know, the first place security will hit. Daringly suicidal."*

"Shut up," she hissed through gritted teeth. The pain in her ankles had graduated from dull throb to screaming agony. "Leo's at the north side. We need to get to him."

"Brilliant," Repip shot back. *"Glad we wasted precious seconds auditioning for a security takedown reel. Next time, maybe open with 'I have a plan.'"*

Piper ducked behind a large family crypt, the stone pressing cold and rough against her spine. She forced her breathing to slow, listening for any sound of pursuit.

"Message Leo," she subvocalized. "Tell him we need immediate extraction. North gate. Security's coming."

"Already on it," Repip replied. *"He's repositioning the car as we speak."*

She peered around the edge of the crypt, scanning the grounds. The cemetery's landscape had transformed from peaceful to threatening. Every shadow could hide a security officer, every sound could be approaching footsteps.

A faint, high-pitched buzz reached her ears, almost imperceptible. *"Got it, analyzing the audio."* Repip's voice was sharp in her head. *"That buzz is an aerial unit—small drone, northwest. The Doppler shift places it within a search grid. In other words, we've been upgraded from 'lucky bystanders' to 'active quarry.'"*

"Crap." Piper pulled back. Open ground stretched between her and the north side, nothing to duck behind except a thin, uneven line of decorative trees, thirty yards out. Their branches formed patchy, uneven darkness along a little winding path. It was her best option.

She pushed off from the crypt, forcing her body into motion despite the protest from her ankles. The sprint across open ground felt endless, every step in plain sight. The drone's faint buzz grew louder, and adrenaline shot through her system.

"Reading its telemetry, standard search grid. Ten seconds before you're center stage. Try not to freeze—spotlights aren't flattering."

Piper lunged forward, diving beneath the tangled web of branches. She hit the ground and rolled hard onto her back, chest heaving. She searched out the patches of sky visible through the bush. The drone passed overhead, its scanning beam sweeping the area she'd just vacated.

"That was unnecessarily athletic," Repip observed.

"Tell me something useful," Piper muttered, pushing herself up. "Where's Leo?"

"He says he is closing on the north gate. One minute out. Which, in case you missed it, is not a lot of minutes."

She started moving again, staying within the tree line. The problem was the north gate. It was still too far, with nothing but open ground to cross.

"Hold up," Repip said sharply. *"Cross-referencing public map with satellite feed... Surprise, the brochure lied. There's a maintenance road a hundred feet ahead, on the right side. It links straight to the north gate's service entrance."*

Piper changed direction, spotting a narrow gravel path cutting between two ornate mausoleums. The maintenance road was almost visible, half-hidden by manicured shrubbery, obviously not meant for visitors. Perfect.

She slipped onto the service path, the gravel crunching beneath her feet. The narrow track wound between utility buildings and groundskeeper sheds, offering both cover and a direct route to the north side.

A sound stopped her cold. Voices ahead, at least two. She flattened herself along the wall of the storage shed, edging closer, then leaned in to peek around the corner.

At the junction where the service road met the wider path to the north gate, two security officers blocked the way. One was a mountain of a man, the other a wiry shape of coiled tension. Their uniforms matched the guard who'd stopped her earlier, but they held themselves differently, tense and alert.

"Any other options?" she subvocalized to Repip.

"No. Every other path costs minutes we don't have. Stick to this one or get caught. Your choice."

Piper assessed the situation. The guards were clustered near a maintenance cart, stuffed with rakes and hedge clippers. The wiry one muttered into his overlay, his voice low and tense, while his larger partner stood guard, gaze sweeping the grounds, one hand resting on the grip of his holstered weapon.

"Repip, new instructions for Leo. Tell him to pull up to the service entrance at the end of *this* road. He needs to be ready to move the second I'm in."

"On it."

"I need a distraction," she whispered.

"Yeah, I'm working on that too," Repip muttered. *"There's a control panel for the irrigation system on the south side of the shed. If you could actually get to it without getting shot, that'd be fantastic..."*

"No time," Piper said. Stone urns were lined up against the shed wall. She gathered her strength. She lunged forward, grabbing an urn. Then she hurled it with everything she had, sending it flying toward the trees on the opposite side of the path.

The urn crashed through the underbrush with a ragged, clattering noise. Both guards snapped around; the large one yanked his weapon free, the other barking fast words into his overlay.

"Go check it out," the large one said, gesturing sharply, taking up position as his partner moved forward. "I'll cover."

As the wiry guard crept closer to the source of the noise, Piper seized her chance. She slipped from her hiding spot and moved swiftly along the wall of the shed, staying in its shadow. The other guard never turned; his focus stayed pinned on his partner and the location of the noise.

The exit to the maintenance area grew closer as she closed the distance—twenty yards, then fifteen, then ten—her heart hammering with each step.

Behind some shrubbery by the exit, the sedan idled with the passenger door propped open. Leo was behind the wheel, his eyes fixed on the path, waiting for her. She was so close.

A barely audible scuff on the gravel sounded behind her.

"The guard is changing direction. Move, now!"

Piper pushed her legs even harder, ignoring the pain in her ankles. Behind her, a shout went up. The sound of running footsteps followed.

"Stop! Security!"

She threw herself into the passenger seat, pulling the door shut as her body was still folding in. "Go!"

The car jerked forward, tires spitting gravel behind them. Piper twisted in her seat, catching a glimpse of the wiry guard, speaking frantically into his overlay.

"Hold on," Leo warned, as the car took the first turn too fast, the back end sliding. Her shoulder slammed into the door as they hit the main cemetery road.

"We need to get to the north gate," she said, fighting to keep her voice steady. "It's our only way out."

Leo nodded and guided the car down the winding cemetery road, picking up speed, the headstones blurring past. The manicured lawns and tidy footpaths didn't even register anymore; now they were just obstacles, hazards, things to be dodged.

"Junction ahead. Left or right?"

"Right," Piper directed. "It'll take us straight to the north entrance."

The car jerked again as Leo took the turn, tires grabbing at the pavement. Piper braced herself, every muscle locked, waiting for headlights in the side mirror, but the road behind stayed clear.

The gate loomed up quick—the iron arch, black and sharp against the sky. The security pillar stood at its side, the gate itself still open. But positioned just inside, a black SUV waited, its engine running, lights off.

"Okay. Exit's blocked," Leo said, his voice remarkably calm.

"Don't stop; just get us close enough and I'll handle the rest."

Leo glanced at her, a question in his eyes, but he didn't slow down. The sedan maintained its speed, barreling toward the gate and the waiting SUV.

"So, what's the grand master plan here?" Repip asked.

"Working on it," Piper muttered.

As they approached the gate, their own headlights washed over the dark SUV, revealing silhouettes stirring inside.

"Slow down," she said to Leo. "Pretend to stop."

Leo eased off the accelerator, and the sedan began to slow, its deceleration carefully measured to give the appearance of surrender.

"Get down," Piper hissed, sliding lower in her seat.

Leo ducked, peering just high enough to see the road, shoulders hunched. The sedan crawled forward, no faster than a slow walk.

She peeked over the window ledge. The SUV's doors swung open. Security personnel were emerging, weapons not drawn but hands ready. They expected compliance—a vehicle stopping for inspection.

"When I say now, floor it and aim for the gap on the left side of the SUV."

They inched closer, the distance between their car and the gate narrowing. Twenty feet. Ten.

"Now!"

Leo slammed the accelerator. The sedan leaped forward and shot toward the narrow space between the SUV and the gate's edge. Security scrambled, bodies lurching for cover, as the sedan knifed through the gap.

Metal screeched against metal. The passenger side of their car scraped along the SUV's bumper, sending shudders through the frame. The gate flashed past, and then they were through, out onto the entry road, which opened ahead on the other side.

"Holy... okay, we're through," Leo said, voice tight but steady as they accelerated away from the cemetery.

Piper kept her eyes on the side mirror, watching for pursuit, but the road behind them remained empty.

"I think we lost them," she said finally, allowing herself to relax marginally against the seat.

"Let's not count our un-arrested chickens just yet," Leo said, his grip on the steering wheel loosening. He rolled his shoulders, a slow, deliberate motion. "How are you holding up?"

She opened her mouth to answer, but Repip cut in, their voice clinical but somehow gentle, *"Cortisol's high but leveling out. Heart rate's back within range. Your ankles are a mess. Strained, not snapped. You'll survive. Probably."*

"Thanks for the medical report," Piper said.

Leo quickly glanced at her. "I feel like I'm missing half the conversation. You wanna fill me in on what your internal co-pilot is saying?"

"Patching our transcript to Leo's overlay," Repip said. *"Looks like he's in the loop now—might as well treat him to the meeting minutes."*

"Great."

"My pleasure," Repip said dryly. *"Would you like a critique of your decision-making now, or should I pencil that in for your next disaster?"*

A small smile tugged at Leo's mouth. "It's nice to see you two have found your rhythm. Even if it's the rhythm of an old married couple who secretly hate each other."

"Let's call it a temporary alliance," Piper said, but there was no bite in her words. The three of them had functioned as a unit, each playing their role without hesitation. It wasn't friendship, but it was something like trust.

She held her breath as they turned onto the city road, the cemetery finally behind them.

"That was too close," Leo said. "Glad we didn't stick around for the cake."

"There wasn't any cake," Piper said, her voice flat... "Instead of being a witness, he gave a lecture on the duty of a superior intellect. He's not an asset, Leo. He's a liability who thinks he's a god."

Leo set the autopilot to his apartment, then met her gaze, his expression hardening. "Well then, let's give him a crisis of faith."

TWENTY-SEVEN

As the car rolled to a stop in the underground parking lot, an adrenaline crash hit Piper harder than she'd expected. Her arms and legs had gone thick and dull, and her brain was foggy. They parked and Leo killed the engine, plunging them into a silence punctuated only by the tick of the cooling engine. They sat without moving, caught in the fluorescent lights that threw clinical shadows across their faces.

"Okay. We're safe for now. Let's get you upstairs," Leo said.

She pushed the door open and eased herself out, wincing as her weight settled onto her injured ankles.

Leo rounded the car and offered his shoulder without a word. She leaned in, letting him take her weight as they moved together toward a steel door. It led to a small service elevator, the kind used for freight and tenant moves.

Behind them, the sedan started up, and its doors closed with a solid thud. Its taillights receded into the darkness as it drove away.

The elevator ride was silent. When the doors slid apart, Leo glanced down the hallway before stepping out. His hand found her side, gentle but certain, guiding her forward.

When they stepped inside Leo's apartment, he didn't just close the door. He twisted the first deadbolt, then the second, and then the third, one after the other, until every lock was snapped into place.

"Standard building security?" Piper asked, arching an eyebrow.

Leo's mouth quirked into a half-smile. "I value my privacy." He walked toward the kitchen, gesturing to the couch as he passed. "How about you get off your feet while I find something frozen for your ankles."

Piper limped toward the couch, and the moment she sank down into it, she let out a long breath. Relief flooded her as the ache in her ankles faded a little. She pushed up the hem of her pant leg. Her ankle had swollen to more than double its usual size and was mottled with ugly shades of purple and yellow.

Leo returned with a bag of frozen green beans and passed it to her without a word. Then he started pacing in front of her. Up and down, a little faster every time.

"So," he said, running a hand through his hair. "Finnagan knew we were coming?"

"Finnagan knew *someone* was coming," she corrected, pressing the green beans against her right ankle. The one that hurt the most. "He didn't know it would be me specifically until I showed up."

"Still," Leo continued, pacing, five steps in one direction, turn, five steps back. "He must have had a security team on standby. That means BOF is watching him closely."

"He said his 'corporate leash' had gotten shorter since our breach." Piper closed her eyes briefly, recalling Finnagan's words. "He basically said Fuller didn't trust him anymore."

"Gee, can't imagine why," Repip chimed in. *"Must be the existential monologues he keeps giving over dead bodies."*

Leo stopped pacing and grabbed the beans from her

ankles. "Okay, this transcript thing is getting inefficient. There's a better way to do this. Come with me."

She grabbed her tablet, and Leo helped her down a short hallway to the bedroom, though calling it a bedroom was like calling an aircraft carrier a boat. The bed was shoved up against one wall, clearly not important. The rest was tech: three huge monitors, all bolted to an arm that looked built for heavy machinery, a brushed-metal desk, and a server rack humming in the corner. Cables hugged the walls, bundled tight, each strand a different color, every inch clipped and tucked away with almost obsessive care.

Piper sat down on the edge of the bed, just looking. The way Leo had things set up was completely over the top, even for a network architect working from home. She'd walked through NSA offices before, seen their rows of cubicles and their gear, and none of it matched what she was staring at now. There was something else: Leo was using an actual computer, not his overlay. Most people his age barely touched keyboards—they did everything through their implants.

"You're not just a network architect. Are you?"

Leo sat down at the desk, fingers already flying across the keyboard. "I am technically employed as a network architect," he replied, not looking up. "Among other things."

"What other things?"

"Let's get Repip online first, then we can swap life stories."

Piper balanced the beans on her ankles; her gaze trailed across the room to the unfamiliar interfaces that Leo navigated, moving rapidly and with surety. Lines of code chased each other down the screen. It was a language she didn't speak.

"Repip," Piper subvocalized. "Are you getting any of this?"

"Only if you keep looking at the screen," Repip said. *"He's rigging a local neural bridge using a hacked radio frequency trans-*

ceiver. Smart. Unauthorized. Completely illegal. I'm starting to really like this guy."

Leo plugged a small device into a port on his desk, then held up what looked like a modified earpiece. "This should let me hear Repip directly," he explained, slipping it into his ear. "And if I route the output through my local comms channel..."

He tapped a few more keys, adjusted a dial on the desk, and nodded with satisfaction.

"Now, while we are in this room, Repip should be able to speak through my system's speakers."

There was a moment of silence, then a voice filled the room. Not Repip's usual sardonic tone, but the smooth, warm cadence of the AI Therapist.

"I notice you're experiencing elevated stress levels. Would you like to try a guided breathing exercise to help regulate your nervous system?"

She froze, her blood turning to ice. "That's not Repip. That's the standard AI Therapist. The last time I stirred BOF up this badly, they sent a tactical team right after. And we just blew through a barricade to escape them."

Leo's hand went instantly to a drawer beside him, pulling it open with controlled urgency.

The voice continued, serene and oblivious. "Let's begin by taking a deep breath in through your nose. Hold for four counts. Now release slowly through your mouth."

Every sound in the apartment suddenly sharpened—the hum of the server rack, the distant city traffic. Her hand went to her hip, fingers finding only empty space. She flattened herself against the wall beside the doorframe, turning her body into a smaller target.

"Oh, that was so worth it," Repip said, snickering. "You should've seen yourselves—confusion, horror, betrayal. Pure art."

Leo's shoulders sagged with relief. Piper exhaled slowly, her heartbeat pounding wild and hard.

"That wasn't funny," she said, but the corner of her mouth twitched upward.

"Disagree," Repip shot back. "It was objectively hilarious. Loved the dramatic drawer reach, by the way—real flair. What's in there? Backup pistol? Pocket EMP? Both feel very on-brand for your 'I'm a spy in tech support' vibe."

Leo closed the drawer without answering, but a large smile had replaced his tension. "Okay. So the comms link works. And Repip's a menace. Good to know."

Repip said, "And I've gotta say, your setup screams professional-grade paranoia. Custom rigs? Triple redundancies? Either you sleep with one eye open, or there's a body buried under this server rack."

"Maybe both," Leo smirked, swiveling in his chair to face Piper. "It's complicated."

"Complicated?" she said, studying him. The adrenaline from Repip's joke had cleared some of the fog from her mind. She saw Leo now with fresh clarity, the pieces not quite fitting together. "You know, for a network architect, you've got some interesting skills."

Leo's expression remained carefully neutral. "I told you. I value my privacy."

"Privacy doesn't explain Thekla, or the Icarus Incident." Piper leaned forward, her investigator instincts fully engaged now. "Who are you really, Leo? Because I'm starting to think network architect is about as accurate as saying I'm just a—"

Piper's words died in her throat; her body locked up, every muscle clenching and trembling. Her legs gave out from under her, and she hit the floor. Pain exploded at the base of her skull and radiated outward, hot, wild, fire crawling through every nerve like it meant to burn her from the inside out.

"Piper!" Leo's voice sounded as if it were coming from very far away.

"Breach!" Repip's voice cut through the pain, sharp with alarm. "They're in the system. BOF is—"

A burst of static interrupted them.

"—found a backdoor. Finnagan must have—"

More static.

"—neural extraction protocol initiated."

Piper couldn't answer. Couldn't budge. The pain wasn't just pain anymore, not really. It had become intimate, more violating. Like someone had dug into her skull and was pulling out bits of her, one piece at a time.

Leo dropped to his knees. "What's happening?" he demanded, his hands on her shoulders, giving her a gentle shake. "Repip! Talk to me!"

"They're pulling me out," Repip's voice fractured, digital artifacts distorting their words. "Targeted extraction. Finnagan gave them the key. He knew exactly where to—"

Leo swore and lunged for his desk, his chair skittering past Piper on the floor. She could hear the frantic clatter of his keyboard.

A piercing squeal cut through the room, feedback from the speakers as Repip's voice stretched and tore. She felt it inside her head, a brutal wrenching as connections tore loose. It wasn't just painful; it was a violation so blunt and deep her mind couldn't even wrap words around it.

Repip's next words came in broken fragments, slowing like a recording losing power. "I hope... they choke on my code..."

And then—nothing. Just a raw, empty silence.

Leo pounded his fist on the desk. "Dammit!"

The pain subsided quickly, like a plug being pulled. Piper sucked air, chest heaving. Things sharpened around her, edges getting crisp. Leo moved to her side, eyes round with worry.

"Repip?" she whispered, reaching instinctively into that corner of her mind where their presence had lived. "Repip, can you hear me?"

Nothing. Only a blankness where Repip had been, a hollow in the world. The loss slammed into her, sharp and sudden. Repip hadn't just been an AI or a program or even a copy of herself. They had been a person, with thoughts and feelings and a distinct consciousness. And now they were gone, ripped away without warning or consent.

"They took Repip," Piper said, her voice breaking. "They just... took them."

Leo's face hardened, and he jumped to his desk. "Maybe there's still a—"

A sound cut him off. Heavy, deliberate, unmistakable.

Someone was pounding on the front door. Not a knock. Ramming.

TWENTY-EIGHT

BOOM. The sound reverberated through the apartment, a blunt shockwave that sent dust raining down from the ceiling. Piper scrambled to her feet, her mind already anticipating a sarcastic comment from Repip. But the space in her head where they had been was still raw and scraped clean.

Leo snatched her by the arm, his fingers digging into her flesh as he hauled her toward the window. As he pulled her, she twisted and snatched her tablet from the bed with her free hand and stuffed it into her waistband.

"Fire escape," he hissed, already moving to the window. His hands worked with practiced efficiency, unlatching locks she hadn't even noticed.

A sharp crack tore through the apartment, piercing the air like a gunshot. It was followed instantly by the pounding of heavy footsteps, too many to count, and moving as one. Not city cops; their rhythm was too coordinated, too focused. This was BOF security.

"Move," Leo said. He shoved the window up. Cold night air

rushed in. He looked back at the bedroom door, listening. "They're clearing rooms. We have maybe fifteen seconds."

The window opened onto a metal landing, the first platform of a zigzagging fire escape that descended the back of the building. Leo climbed out first. He turned, steady hands reaching for her, sliding under her arms. She felt him hold her weight, careful as she dragged her legs through the window. Leo didn't let go until she was balanced, both of them breathing hard on the landing.

"They're coming," she whispered, hearing the systematic opening of doors down the hallway. Closer now. Seconds away.

The bedroom door slammed open a split second after Leo yanked the window closed. Through the glass, Piper caught a flicker of black tactical gear, the BOF logo stamped boldly on chest plates.

Leo pushed her toward the metal stairs. The fire escape creaked beneath them, each step a betrayal of their location. She gripped the cold railing, trying to distribute her weight away from her throbbing ankles.

A shout echoed from above as the window slammed open.

Leo half-dragged, half-carried Piper, metal steps clanging under his boots. Three flights to go. Two. The alley below was a rectangle of darkness cut between buildings, impossibly far away. Above them, more boots, tactical, heavy, hitting steel.

"I can't go any faster," she gasped, her ankles sending shards of pain up her legs with each step.

"You don't have to," Leo replied, and hoisted her over his shoulder in a fireman's carry. The world tilted sickeningly as he descended the last flight at dangerous speed, the metal steps ringing with each impact.

He reached the bottom landing and set her down, scanning the alley below. The final ladder was fixed in place, with no drop-down mechanism. They'd have to climb down.

"I'll go first," he said. "I'll catch you at the bottom."

He swung over the railing and disappeared down the ladder. Piper followed immediately, ignoring the pain in her ankles as she gripped the cold metal rungs. One rung, then the next. Don't look up. Don't look down.

A bullet pinged off the metal right next to her head. A quick, sharp note, slicing the air in half. The world snapped into hyper-focus. A jolt of pure adrenaline surged through her, a chemical fire that erased the pain in her ankles, replacing it with a buzzing, electric urgency.

She didn't freeze. Didn't hesitate. She let go.

The fall was brief, but it stretched on forever. Then Leo caught her, absorbing the impact with a grunt. He staggered and then set her on her feet in one fluid motion.

"Run," he said, turning toward the mouth of the alley. His hand landed on the small of her back, a firm, urgent push that sent her stumbling forward. The adrenaline was a fire in her veins, and she ran through a pain that now felt distant and unimportant.

They burst from the alley's confines onto a deserted side street, and her overlay map oriented instantly. Three blocks east was the night market, a sprawling maze of stalls and crowds where they could disappear. She nodded east and they ran while she led the way.

Bullets cracked against the pavement behind them. The tactical team wasn't firing to kill. They wanted them alive.

One block down. A sharp stitch stabbed into her side, a fire that knotted her muscles with every stride.

Two blocks. Her lungs burned, not from exertion but from the cold night air scraping down her throat in ragged gulps.

Pressure built behind her eyes, a vise tightening around her skull. She stumbled, her stride breaking.

"No," she gasped. "Not now." But her body didn't care about

timing or survival or the tactical team closing in behind them. The fog descended, ruthless and absolute.

The world fragmented. Sound separated from vision. Colors detached from shapes. Her sense of balance vanished, leaving her adrift in a sea of conflicting sensory input. Her muscles locked, and she came to a sudden halt mid-stride.

She felt the pull of gravity and a brief tilt. Then, without warning, the ground shot up fast and connected with her in a muted explosion of pain.

Leo's voice reached her through layers of distortion, "Piper? Piper!"

She couldn't respond. Couldn't move. Her body was a failed instrument, refusing the most basic commands. Through the storm of broken sensory data, she was aware of Leo kneeling beside her, his hands on her shoulders, trying to lift her.

"Get up, Piper, please. You have to. They're right behind us."

The words lined up in her mind, but no matter how hard she tried, they didn't cross the space between knowing and doing. Her arms, her legs—they stayed still, trapped in the neural misfire that Repip had called "permanent scarring."

Gradually, agonizingly, the fog began to recede. First her fingers, then her arms responded to her will. But she was recovering too slowly. She managed to turn her head, vision clearing. At the far end of the street, a tactical team was advancing on their position. They moved in a tight, disciplined formation, using parked cars for cover as they systematically closed the distance.

"Go," she managed, the word slurred and thick. "Run."

Leo shook his head, a quick, decisive motion. "Not happening."

"Please," she begged, the fog lifting enough for desperation to break through. "Don't let them take you too."

Something shifted in Leo's face then—a spark of panic,

replaced, almost instantly, by resolve. He squeezed her shoulder, just once, and then stood.

"Get to the market," he said, his voice oddly calm. "I'll meet you there. I'm going to create a distraction."

Piper reached for him, grabbed at empty air, as he twisted away, ducked, and ran toward the tactical team moving in.

"No." It came out as a whisper, but he was already gone. The fog kept lifting, piece by piece, until she could feel her body again. She got to her knees, hands planted, then forced herself to stand. She wobbled, shaky on her feet.

Leo stopped in the middle of the street, hands raised high, fingers spread. The tactical team slowed, their weapons leveled at him, their steps measured and deliberate. He was speaking, mouth forming words, but she couldn't catch them—just the steady, practiced rhythm of his voice floating back, clipped and sure.

He was sacrificing himself so she could escape. The knowledge galvanized her. She wouldn't waste it. So she turned. Pushed her body forward. Awkward at first, but then steadier, surer, as the last of the fog peeled away. Shouting behind her. A struggle. And then a sharp command cut through the air behind her—"Runner, east side!"—and a new set of footsteps broke from the main group, pounding the pavement behind her. She didn't look back. Couldn't. Looking back meant stopping. And stopping meant capture.

The market appeared ahead, a constellation of lights and noise spilling onto the street. She risked a glance over her shoulder—the black-clad figure was closing, maybe fifty yards back, cutting through the traffic. With a final, desperate burst of speed, she plunged into the chaos, the sheer density of the weekend crowd a welcome, suffocating shield.

She didn't run in a straight line. She weaved between stalls selling everything from produce to counterfeit tech. Then she ducked under a vendor's awning and used a slow-moving group of tourists as temporary cover, letting the current of bodies carry her deeper into the labyrinth. The shouts of her pursuer grew more distant, muffled by the market's own cacophony of vendors hawking wares. After three more sharp turns down narrow, steam-filled aisles, she risked a final look back.

Nothing. The human tide had closed behind her, swallowing her trail whole. Only then was she certain she'd lost him. In a narrow aisle between food stalls, she finally allowed herself to pause, ducking into the shadow behind a vendor's stall, its bamboo steamers stacked high and billowing fragrant clouds.

The sweet, savory smell of the steaming buns hit her, and a sharp, painful hunger pang twisted in her gut. It was another cruel joke. Her body, a machine, still mimicking the desperate needs of the humanity she felt she'd lost. She closed her eyes. Breathe in. Hold it. Out. Again. In, hold, out.

The grief hit, sudden and solid; a punch that drove every breath from her chest, and a single, choked sob broke from her lips as Leo's face swam in her memory. Leo was gone. Taken. All because of her.

If she hadn't frozen. If this damned foreign body hadn't failed her at the critical moment, they both would have made it. A real human wouldn't have short-circuited. A real partner wouldn't have let him go. The image of him walking toward the tactical team, hands up without hesitation, was a fresh and brutal torment.

It wasn't just Leo who was gone. Repip was gone too, not even a whisper left behind. The emptiness felt jagged and cold, as if a part of her mind had been sliced out. She gasped, a ragged, silent breath, as if the air itself had been stolen from her lungs, and pressed the back of her hand hard against her mouth.

She looked up through blurry, tear-filled eyes at the river of life flowing past the narrow opening, completely unaware of the wreckage inside her.

She was invisible here, another shadow among shadows, watching a world that had no idea.

Piper shut her eyes. Let the truth roll over her. The system couldn't help her. The institutions she had served and believed in were either corrupted or powerless against what she faced. There would be no backup, no extraction team, and no friends to rescue her. She was completely, terrifyingly on her own.

A soft shuffling sound nearby made her flinch, ready for a threat.

It was the steamed bun vendor, an old woman with deep-set, tired eyes and flour dusting her apron. Piper instinctively tried to shrink further into the shadows. She was suddenly and painfully aware of the tear tracks on her face, the way she held herself pressed into the shadows like a cornered animal.

Without a word, the woman turned back to her stall. A moment later, she returned, holding out a fresh bun wrapped in paper. Steam still curled from its folds, a small offering of warmth.

She stared at it, her training screaming at her not to trust, not to take anything from a stranger. She shook her head, a tiny, negative gesture.

The old woman's gaze flickered past her, out into the crowded aisle, then back to Piper's face. The tiredness in her eyes sharpened for a moment into something else: understanding. She pushed the bun a little closer, her expression gentle but insistent. Then, she gave a small, almost imperceptible jerk of her head toward the back of her stall.

"Rest," the vendor whispered.

That one word broke her. A tremor started in her hand and spread through her entire body, a violent, silent shudder of a dam breaking inside. She reached out, took the bun, and felt the warmth seep into her cold, trembling fingers.

She met the old woman's eyes, her throat so tight with unshed grief that no sound could escape.

The vendor simply patted her hand once, a brief, papery touch, before turning back to her stall.

Piper looked from the warm bun in her hand to the curtained-off darkness behind the counter. After a heartbeat of indecision, she slipped past the woman and pushed aside the heavy canvas curtain. The space behind it was small and dark, smelling of cardboard and something faintly sweet. The noise of the market was a muffled, distant hum.

She leaned back against a stack of boxes, holding the warm bun in her hand. She was still alone, still hunted. But hidden in the small, anonymous sanctuary a stranger had provided, she felt, for the first time all night, a pinprick of warmth in the vast, cold emptiness.

TWENTY-NINE

Dawn broke in thin, watery strips across the eastern sky, washing the park in a gray light. Familiar shapes emerged from the darkness —benches, trees, the distant outline of buildings—but everything felt strange, unreal. The rough stone of the fountain's rim bit into the backs of Piper's thighs, while the water lapped at her ankles, a cold caress that had numbed the pain hours ago.

She'd been here since 3 AM, after zigzagging through the city until her legs nearly gave out. Then, when the security patrols thinned, she slipped into the park. Not the safest choice. But safer than anywhere else.

Sleep had come in broken fragments. Twenty minutes curled under a hedge against the cold. Then maybe an hour beneath the sag of a willow, its curtain of leaves pretending at shelter. Later, she sat by the fountain, where she gave up on sleep and dipped her feet into the cold water.

She couldn't go home. That much was certain. Her apartment would be the first place they'd look, if they weren't already there, waiting. Her bed, her shower, clean clothes—all of it now forbidden territory.

Her world had shrunk to this cold stone edge and a fountain full of murky water.

A maintenance bot zipped along the main path fifty yards off, dutifully following its route, programmed to ignore the little hidden spot where she sat. Small mercies. She wiggled her toes in the water, and sensation prickled back with a sharp edge, making her wince. The swelling was down. The damage, though, lingered —a narrow band of pain cinched tight around both ankles.

"Repip?" she tried again, the word swallowed by the pre-dawn quiet.

Nothing answered. Only the low, gurgling splash of the fountain, and the city's hum, stirring somewhere beyond the park's edge.

Her stomach twisted, a queasy combination of the hollow ache in her head where Repip had been and the fresh, sharp grief for Leo. The thought of what BOF was doing to them both was enough to make her double over, arms wrapped tight around her middle as if to hold herself together.

"I'm sorry," she whispered to the sky, an apology neither Leo nor Repip could hear.

She hadn't known Leo long, but it was long enough to see the hints of a hidden past, to know "network architect" was a pitiful cover. It had been long enough to watch him risk everything for her, without a moment's hesitation. The questions about who he was or what the Icarus Incident meant felt pointless now. He'd chosen her side, and now he was paying for it.

This was all her fault.

If she hadn't pursued the case, if she hadn't followed the trail to BOF, if she hadn't contacted Leo—then maybe all of this would never have happened.

But that wasn't fair, either. BOF had started this, not her. They'd built a program to manipulate people without consent.

They'd killed Anna Moreau and her child. They'd made Repip a tortured experiment. All she had been doing was her job, following the evidence, letting it take her where it wanted.

Still, the guilt pressed down on her, solid—a weight she couldn't shake. She shifted on the edge of the fountain, searching for a spot that might not hurt, but it was useless. Her body had passed a critical threshold of exhaustion where everything ached with a bone-deep fatigue.

She knew what she should do: get up, find food, seek shelter, and figure out a plan. But it felt pointless. So she stayed put, staring at the water as it shifted and caught the light, determined not to think about anything at all.

A notification pinged in her overlay, loud enough to cut through the hush of morning. Her heart jumped. A notification meant people, and right now, people meant danger.

But this wasn't a message. It was a news alert, automated, pushed through some algorithm that decided she needed to know about it: "Behavioral Optimization Firm Exec Named in Flow Scandal."

For a moment, she stared at the headline, not comprehending. Then she opened the full article. The words swam in front of her tired eyes. She forced herself to focus. To parse the corporate speak and journalist hedging.

Dr. Ray Finnagan, Senior Architect at the Behavioral Optimization Firm, has been terminated following allegations of unauthorized data manipulation in the company's Flow app. In a statement released early this morning, BOF's CEO Lathem Fuller expressed "profound disappointment" in Finnagan's "gross negligence" and assured users that a patch addressing all identified issues is being deployed.

"The integrity of our products and the trust of our users are paramount," Fuller stated. "The unauthorized modifications made by Dr. Finnagan were a betrayal of that trust. We are implementing enhanced oversight protocols to ensure such a breach never happens again."

Dr. Finnagan was not available for comment. Sources inside the company describe the termination as "immediate and non-negotiable."

The Flow app, a beta wellness program designed to help users manage anxiety and improve focus, has been the subject of growing concern following user reports of unusual behavioral changes. BOF maintains that these issues were limited to a small test group and will be fully resolved by the upcoming patch.

A surge of helpless anger made her snatch a loose rock from the fountain's edge and hurl it at the spout. It just plinked off, a small, unsatisfying sound. This was their play. Pin everything on Finnagan. Make the behavioral changes look like the blunder of a lone employee, not a calculated, profit-driven scheme. Push out a "patch" that would do nothing to stop the manipulation, just bury it deeper and make it even harder to find.

They weren't shutting down Flow. They were streamlining it.

A phrase from Fuller's statement echoed in her head: "limited to a small test group." A bitter, humorless laugh escaped her lips. *Small?* She knew of at least three cases—Anna Moreau, the compulsive minimalist, the woman who flew to Greece. And those were the ones she'd stumbled upon. How many others were there? How many people, just walking around, Flow in their heads, being nudged to buy junk, to say yes to things they'd never have considered?

She closed the article with a sharp gesture. The whole thing was a corporate sleight of hand, designed to make the public feel safe while BOF continued its predatory practices. The idea that BOF would actually fire the architect of Flow was laughable. They needed him too much.

Unless...

She blinked hard. What if Finnagan had actually crossed a line? Not with Flow itself—that was always the plan—but with her. With Project Cadence. With the way he'd forked her consciousness. Maybe that was one step too far, even for BOF. Or maybe it was just too big a liability.

It didn't matter. What mattered was that BOF was covering their tracks, burying the evidence, making sure the money kept flowing. They would keep manipulating people, keep violating autonomy, keep playing god with human minds. Only now they'd get better at hiding it.

Something shifted inside her, like gears finally catching, locking onto a new track, cutting through the grief. The grief and guilt didn't disappear—they clung to her ribs, pressed against her lungs—but they shuffled, scooted over, left a pocket for something else. Purpose. A mission.

She couldn't bring Repip back. Leo was still out of reach, for now. But BOF? She could stop them from doing this to anyone else. She could put everything out in the open, not just for the OAA, but for everyone to see. She could make sure the whole world knew what BOF was really doing inside their heads.

The sun peeked over the horizon, casting shadows that skimmed long and thin across the park. Piper drew her feet up and out of the water, wincing as she set them down, testing her weight on her battered ankles. The pain had dulled enough to bear. She straightened, bit by bit, keeping her balance.

For the first time since the chase, since losing Repip, since watching Leo walk away, she felt a kind of clarity. The world had narrowed to a single point. BOF expected her to run. But she had nothing left to lose, and that made her dangerous.

THIRTY

Piper stood across the street from the concrete slab that was Rossi's precinct, her body pressed into the shadow of a shuttered bodega. Morning had broken now, the city waking with a groan. Delivery trucks barreled by, and office workers clutched coffee cups like they might drown without them. Nobody looked at her, not even twice, though she probably looked like hell.

Rossi had been her partner for three years. That was long enough to know which jokes would make her smile on a bad day. Long enough to develop a kind of shorthand, something that skipped past words completely. Long enough to trust him with her life, and she'd done it, more than once. But this wasn't about her life anymore. This was about Leo and Repip and every person who had Flow installed. The question wasn't whether she trusted Rossi. It was whether she could justify pulling him into this mess with her. But there was only one path left open to her, and it led right to him.

Rossi would be here. He liked to come in early, before the day shift really got rolling, to ease into his day. She'd teased him about it once. Called him a creature of habit. He'd shrugged, that loose, easy motion of his shoulders, and said, "Dead people don't care what time of day it is."

She picked a spot by the staff entrance, wedged herself in between a support column and a department sedan. From this angle, the door was in full view, but she stayed mostly out of sight. She should abort, turn back right now. Rossi had a family, a mortgage, a pension. All of it at risk if BOF decided he was a threat. But she couldn't stop BOF from violating everyone by herself. She needed help.

She messaged Rossi on her tablet.

> Need to talk. Side door. Now. Life or death. – P

She waited.

After seven minutes, the door swung open, but it wasn't Rossi. It was a young patrol officer who walked by, his attention fixed on his phone, completely oblivious. Piper didn't move, and he passed without a second glance.

The door creaked open. Rossi stepped out. His hair was now more salt than pepper, thinner at the temples. The lines on his face had deepened since she saw him last. Still, he moved with that same easy grace—a man at home in his skin.

She stepped out from her hiding place, just enough for him to see her. Recognition showed on his face, chased immediately by worry.

He reached her in three long strides, crowding her back into the shadows and using his bulk to shield her from view.

"Jesus, Cadence," he muttered. "What the hell are you doing here?"

Up close, the dark circles under his eyes were stark, the stubble on his jaw rough and graying. He looked tired. Worn down.

"Rossi," she started, her voice cracking on his name. "I need help. I need you to listen to what I have to say."

His eyes were still sharp, and she felt their focus sweep over her, cataloging everything.

"You look like hell," he said, but his voice had softened. "When's the last time you slept? Or ate?"

"That's not important right now."

"Like hell it isn't." He glanced around, checking for witnesses. "We can't talk here. Too exposed."

He was right. Cameras were everywhere in the parking structure. People drifting in, drifting out.

"I know a place," he said. "Around back. Maintenance keeps equipment there, but nobody uses it this time of day."

She nodded, letting him lead the way. They moved fast, staying close to the wall. Rossi was a half-step ahead, his walk loose, almost lazy. Just a detective, taking the side entrance, nothing special here.

The maintenance room was barely even a closet, jammed floor to ceiling with bottles, rags, and random pieces of equipment. Industrial cleaner hung in the air, sharp and sour. Rossi closed the door and turned to face her.

"Alright, Cadence. Talk. You've got five minutes before I'm missed."

The story came out in a torrent, a desperate, jumbled confession. The Flow program. Behavioral manipulations. Anna Moreau and her daughter. Repip. Leo. The truth about what she was—an android. She laid it all out for him, detail after detail, her words tumbling over each other, faster and faster, like if she just kept going, he'd have to believe her. And through it all, he only watched, face unreadable, a professional mask, the one he kept on when he didn't want anyone to know what he was thinking.

When she finished, the silence stretched between them, elastic and taut. He studied her for a long moment, eyes narrowed, hands in his pockets.

"That's... quite a story," he said finally, each word measured, precise.

"It's not a story." Her hands clenched at her sides. "It's what happened. It's still happening."

Rossi leaned against a shelf, letting out a sigh, tired and heavy. "Listen," he said, rubbing at his forehead, "I want to believe you. Really. But you're telling me a big corporation is out there mind-controlling people, and then there's this whole conspiracy on top of it, all hush-hush. That's... that's a lot. Even for me."

"I have proof," she said, reaching for her tablet. "The Project Cadence file—"

"Don't." His voice had an edge now, sharp enough to cut. "Don't show me anything. Don't implicate me."

She froze. Something had shifted in his demeanor, a subtle withdrawal, a stepping back even though he hadn't moved.

"What aren't you telling me?" she asked, the words barely audible.

Rossi ran a hand through his thinning hair, a gesture so familiar it made her chest ache. "There's an alert out for you. Department-wide. You're wanted for questioning in connection with a corporate espionage investigation."

"That's bull—"

"I know what it is," he cut her off. "But it's official. Came down from the Commissioner's office yesterday. You're a person of interest in the unauthorized access of BOF's secure servers and the dissemination of sensitive information."

The words hit her like physical blows, each one landing with precision. "They're framing me."

"They're saying you hacked into the company's system and stole proprietary code. That you've been selling it to competitors.

That the complaints you filed were a smokescreen to cover your tracks."

The air in the small maintenance room suddenly felt too thick to breathe.

"And people believe that? People who know me?"

His expression softened, just a fraction. "Not everyone. But enough. The evidence they've presented is... compelling."

"Fabricated."

"Maybe." He looked away, focusing on a point just past her shoulder. "But it's there. And it's legal. And it's backed by witness statements and digital forensics and a paper trail a mile long."

"Rossi." She took a step forward, closing the gap between them. "You know me. You know I wouldn't—"

"I thought I knew you." The words were quiet, almost gentle. "But the Piper Cadence I knew wouldn't break into secure facilities. Wouldn't hack private servers. Wouldn't go rogue and disappear for days without contacting anyone."

"I couldn't. They're watching—"

"Listen to yourself." There was genuine concern in his voice now, mixed with something else, pity. "Surveillance. Conspiracies. Mind control. Do you know how that sounds?"

She did. She knew exactly how it sounded. Paranoid and delusional. The ravings of someone who'd lost touch with reality.

"They have Leo," she said, a final, desperate appeal. "They took Repip. They're in people's heads, Rossi. They're manipulating them, and no one can see it because it's subtle. It feels natural. Like it's your own idea."

Rossi's expression closed off entirely, his face returning to that professional mask. "I think you should turn yourself in. Come in with me. We'll talk to the captain together. Then we'll get you a lawyer and do this the right way."

Even knowing the odds, she'd allowed a small sliver of hope

that Rossi would surprise her, that their shared past would count for more than nothing.

"I can't do that."

"Piper." He rarely used her first name. It struck her like a slap. "If you walk out that door, I'm obligated to report this. To tell them you were here. That you contacted me."

She nodded, understanding. He was giving her a head start. A small mercy, but a mercy nonetheless.

"Thank you for listening," she said, reaching for the door.

"Wait." He caught her arm, his grip firm but not painful. "Whatever you're planning, whatever you think you're going to do... be careful. These people—if even half of what you're saying is true—they won't hesitate to bury you."

"I know." She managed a small, bitter smile. "They already have."

She slipped out the door and made it out of the parking structure without being spotted, threading her way through the morning traffic, just another face in the crowd. She walked without direction, putting distance between herself and the precinct, between herself and the last thread of her old life.

Every legitimate avenue was closed now. The police, the OAA, her colleagues—all of them were dead ends.

She stopped dead on the sidewalk. A businessman had to jerk around her, muttering something sharp under his breath.

What she knew couldn't be a secret, not something whispered to officials who could be silenced or bought off. No, this had to be loud. She needed to throw the facts out in the open where everyone could see.

For that, she needed a journalist.

THIRTY-ONE

Piper sat in the laundromat with her tablet balanced on her knees, while the dryer spun her sweatshirt in endless, drowsy circles. The fluorescent lights gave everything a washed-out, sickly cast. An old man folding shirts with perfect, careful movements. A half-asleep college kid slumped behind a textbook. A tired mother wrangled a toddler, sorting clothes one-handed. No one so much as glanced at her. She was just a woman, doing laundry. Anonymous. Forgettable.

Without her sweatshirt, goosebumps prickled along her arms. Her t-shirt was not enough protection against the air conditioning set to Arctic. The discomfort was a small price for normalcy. For the appearance of someone with nowhere better to be, no urgent mission, just dirty clothes, just time to kill.

Twenty-seven minutes until her sweatshirt was dry. Twenty-seven minutes to make her pitch.

Her fingers hovered above the tablet, just shy of the screen. The journalist's contact info stared back at her: Acvina Teller, Investigative Reporter, The Daily. Four years ago, she'd slipped Acvina a tip about evidence tampering. Acvina had played it smart, kept Piper insulated as a source. That had to mean something now, didn't it?

But this wasn't a friendly tip about departmental corruption; this was an accusation of a corporate conspiracy so vast it dealt in mind control and murder, with thousands of lives on the line. And she had almost nothing solid to show for it.

A crash in the corner made her shoulders jerk. The toddler had toppled a basket of clothes and laundry soap. The mother exhaled and stooped to gather the scattered clothes. Piper forced the tension from her shoulders. It wasn't a threat from BOF's security, at least not yet.

She had to be more careful. She moved to the windows. There wasn't anything outside. No strange car or men standing too straight, a jacket pulled over where a weapon might hide. Just the usual morning traffic, cars rolling by, and people moving along.

She forced her focus to the dryer. Each lazy, endless tumble of her sweatshirt was a second slipping away. Twenty-five minutes left. That was all.

She began typing, choosing her words with precision.

> Acvina. Piper Cadence. The story BOF is selling about Finnagan is a lie. He wasn't a rogue employee; he was the scapegoat. I have evidence that the Flow program's manipulation was a corporate-wide strategy approved by CEO Lathem Fuller, and that their 'patch' is just a deeper cover-up. It's already led to deaths. Need to meet, securely.

She hit send before she could second-guess herself.

The message disappeared into the digital void. Piper's chest tightened. What if they were monitoring communications? What if they were already tracing this? She forced herself to breathe. One problem at a time. Right now, she needed to wait.

The elderly man smoothed his last shirt, tucked it into a canvas bag, and shuffled to the door. The bell above chimed—a bright, brittle note as it swung shut behind him. Piper watched through the window as he made his slow way down the street, then rounded the corner and vanished.

Her tablet pinged.

> Piper? This is unexpected. And frankly, concerning. You're listed as AWOL from the department, possibly involved in corporate espionage. Are you safe? And more importantly, are you sure about these allegations? BOF is not a company to cross lightly.

Her pulse ratcheted up. Acvina hadn't laughed at her. That had to count for something.

Her fingers flew across the tablet, laying out everything in a torrent of text—the fabricated espionage charges, Flow's true purpose as a manipulation tool, the Moreau case, and BOF's cover-up that framed Finnagan to protect the real person in charge: CEO Lathem Fuller.

> That's a massive accusation. I need more than your word, even with our history. What kind of documentation are we talking about?

Piper's stomach twisted. This was the part she'd been dreading. How could she explain Repip? The corrupted file? That her best evidence had been stolen, and the rest was scattered fragments, broken and incomplete?

I accessed internal BOF files and started downloading them. But at about 80 percent, security locked me out. The file is corrupted, but it shows their research. And my primary source... Well, BOF captured them during my escape. They were a sentient AI.

An AI? You're saying your main source is an artificial intelligence?

Yes. A fork of my own consciousness was created during a procedure I did not consent to. They were helping me expose BOF, and they had direct access to the firm's servers.

As she hit send, she could almost hear how it sounded. The college student stirred, mumbled something, then settled back to sleep.

Piper, given our history, I believe you. But I need you to hear me, not as a friend, but as a journalist. I cannot publish a story based on a corrupted file and the testimony of a sentient AI, who you yourself say has been captured. My editor wouldn't just laugh me out of the building; the legal team would have a coronary. BOF would bury this paper in lawsuits before the ink was dry. Without a verifiable human source—a whistleblower, someone on record— or a complete, uncompromised document, all you have is a story. And I can't risk my career, and this paper's existence, on a story I can't prove.

She stared at the words on the screen. The hollow, endless thump of the dryer filled the laundromat, each rotation landing like a nail being hammered into a coffin.

Forget it. I shouldn't have contacted you.
Delete this conversation. For your own safety.

I'm sorry, Piper. Truly. If you find something
concrete, contact me again. Until then, please
consider getting help. Whatever's happening,
you don't have to face it alone.

She *was* alone. Utterly and completely. Even her last hope had
turned her away.

THIRTY-TWO

■■■ ■■■■■ ■ ■■■■ ■■■■ ■ ■■■

The mother with the toddler gathered her laundry and left, the bell above the door chiming their exit. The college kid snored in the corner while his dryer tumbled on. In the sickly fluorescent light of the laundromat, Piper read the journalist's final rejection again, and the last door in her world quietly clicked shut. The snore from the corner and the rhythmic churn of the dryer went on, indifferent, while her world contracted around the rejection on her screen.

Her fingers hovered above the tablet. The corrupted file sat in her storage, labeled with an icon marked "Project Cadence 82%." Not enough proof for Acvina. Not enough for anyone.

But she'd seen the evidence with her own eyes, felt Flow's directives, the subtle pressure, the attempt to nudge her thinking. This was real.

But reality without proof was just a story. And stories couldn't save Leo or bring Repip back. Stories couldn't stop BOF.

She tapped the Project Cadence icon and the file opened into the same chaos as before: corrupted data, splintered text, broken images, long slabs of hexadecimal. She had combed it again and again, salvaging the few legible scraps, yet still nothing anyone would call proof.

But maybe she'd been looking for the wrong thing.

As a detective, she'd learned that sometimes the most valuable evidence wasn't the thing you could point at: the weapon, the body, the bloodstain. Sometimes it was the thing that should have been there but wasn't.

She closed her eyes and focused. What was she missing? What hadn't she asked?

Finnagan had been doing illegal research for years, experimenting on Repip in secret. He'd been communicating with Repip, running simulations. But how? If the Project was hidden, if it was his private, forbidden work, he wouldn't have used BOF's regular channels. He'd have needed something secure, something untraceable.

Her eyes snapped open. A communication procedure.

Her fingers steadied. The helplessness thinned, replaced by the rhythm of work. She wasn't searching for proof anymore; she was searching for a hidden line Finnagan may have used. Some sort of trace that would reveal a backdoor. A way back in.

She tapped her tablet and set the search parameters for external communication, adding Finnagan's developer ID from the project files. Then she narrowed the timeframe to the period when he was actively working on Project Cadence and tapped the search button.

The college student's dryer beeped, cycle complete, but she didn't look up; her eyes stayed on the screen as the search filtered the corrupted data, dumping gibberish and stitching fragments together.

She heard the clatter of the dryer door, the rustle of clothes being dumped into a garbage bag, and a moment later, the bell above the main door chimed. The algorithm continued to comb through the data. For a long moment, it seemed like a dead end. Then a single hit: Comms Test Log.

She tapped it, heart rate picking up. The file opened, mostly corrupted, blocks of nonsensical characters punctuated by rare, readable fragments. She scrolled slowly, methodically, scanning for anything useful.

Midway through, a line of developer notes, preserved somehow in the chaos:

//Testing Inbound Message Functionality. Partition-R Response Verified. Logging Enabled for Diagnostic Purposes Only.//

Below it, a partial log entry:

Inbound Transmission... Source ID: JHf7$R*2!9pQ@Lm^K3sZ... Destination ID: P-R

She jolted, the tablet nearly slipping from her lap. P-R. That was Repip—"Partition-R"—the name that had appeared in the BOF diagnostic, the "legacy artifact" that had fascinated Finnagan.

Her pulse quickened. This wasn't noise; it was Finnagan's developer key, the credential he used to message commands to Repip. His backdoor into the simulation, left behind from an experiment years ago.

And if it existed once...

She sat very still, letting the realization settle. Finnagan had been sending messages. Which meant there was a path. A channel. And if it existed once, it could be a way to reach him.

Her mouth went dry. Her hands trembled above the tablet.

Was she really considering this? Reaching out to Finnagan? The man who had violated her very existence, who had treated Repip like a lab rat, who had helped create the Flow program that had killed Anna Moreau and her child?

But who else was there? The police wouldn't help. The journalist couldn't publish without proof. Even Rossi, her former partner, thought she'd lost her mind.

Finnagan was the only other person on Earth who knew the full truth. Who had the technical understanding? Who might, just might, have a reason to help her now that BOF had cast him out.

This wasn't a good idea. It was her last option, but it was still an option.

Resigned to it, she took her sweatshirt out of the dryer and pulled it on, but the lingering warmth provided no comfort for what she was about to do.

She tapped the tablet and pulled up the secure messaging channel. It was almost identical to the comms app used by officers to talk to handlers. The interface looked the same, and the messaging key wasn't so different from the ones she'd just discovered.

She set the tablet on her lap. If she did this, there was no going back. She'd be opening a line to the architect of her nightmare, the man who had played god with her existence.

But if she didn't, BOF would win. They'd bury the truth. They'd keep Flow running, keep manipulating people. Leo would remain their prisoner. And Repip—whatever was left of them— would stay in BOF's digital clutches.

With a final, bitter exhale, her fingers trembling with a mixture of rage and defeat, she copied the key, pasted it into the correct field, and typed.

> BOF made you the public villain. They made me a fugitive. They think we're both neutralized. They're wrong. We can burn Fuller to the ground together, or I can release everything I have and make sure we both go down in flames. Your call.

She hit send, hoping he wouldn't call her bluff.

The message went out on a path so old and encrypted she didn't know if it would even arrive.

But it was something. It was action. It was the last door in the universe.

And Piper had just knocked.

THIRTY-THREE

———————————

The diner smelled of burnt coffee and cheap disinfectant, a greasy film clinging to every surface. Piper sat in the corner booth, back to the wall, exit in sight. A cop's habit, but she wasn't one anymore. She was a fugitive, a loose thread BOF was coming to snip. She checked her overlay. Twenty minutes had passed since she'd sent the message, and she'd almost walked out four times.

She shifted, wincing as her ankles bumped the table leg. The swelling had at least subsided, and the pain was now manageable. Not healed, but functional. Good enough to run, if she had to.

A waiter drifted by with a coffee pot in hand, a question in his raised eyebrows. Piper nodded. He poured, and the coffee splashed darkly into the cup, as steam lifted in thin ribbons. She wrapped her hands around the mug, letting the heat seep into her palms.

A draft of cold from the door sliced the air, sharp and sudden. Piper looked up.

Finnagan moved with that same odd gait she'd seen at the cemetery, leaning back, always a little on his heels. As if he were trying to hover above everything, forming opinions as he went. The outfit was different too; no longer high-end, fashion-forward.

He wore a simple gray sweater, dark slacks, and practical shoes. Camouflage for a man suddenly thrust from privilege into caution.

He dropped into the booth across from her, every move measured, not a single twitch out of place. His face looked narrower than it had the last time, his skin drawn tight over sharp cheekbones, giving his gray eyes an even more pronounced intensity.

"Investigator Cadence. Or shall I say just Cadence, since you've been relieved of your duties."

The rage hit fast—a quick, ugly bloom that flared in her chest and started to climb. She forced it down and smoothed her face, because everything depended on her staying calm. "Dr. Finnagan. Considering you're supposedly terminated, you look remarkably composed."

His mouth twitched, not quite a smile, just an acknowledgment that her barb had landed. "So that's what Lathem is telling people? That I've been 'terminated'? It lacks imagination, don't you think? But then, so does he." He placed a hand on the table as if to make a point. "And yet, you came looking for me. Which suggests you suspect the official narrative is... incomplete."

"I reached out because I need something from you." She leaned forward, lowering her voice. "And you need something from me."

"A symbiotic relationship? Do elaborate." A small, condescending smile played at the corners of his mouth.

"You need revenge. BOF threw you to the wolves, made you the public face of their 'bug.' Said you were acting alone and that it was your fault."

Something flickered in his eyes. A brief, sharp flash, there and gone in an instant. She'd hit a nerve. Good.

"Revenge is such an emotional, imprecise term. I prefer accountability. But you, my dear Cadence? What is it you need?"

"Proof." She kept her voice low and steady. "Proof that Flow was never a bug, that it was designed to manipulate users. That Fuller knew, approved it, and sold behavioral modifications to the highest bidder."

"And then what?" Finnagan asked, arching an eyebrow. "After you have this proof? What is the desired outcome?"

"I expose it. All of it. BOF and Fuller go down. The whole operation gets dismantled."

"Your objective is laudable. Your methodology, however, is fatally flawed. You are a null set, Cadence. A fugitive with a compromised reputation. Your testimony is inadmissible noise."

Under the table, she twisted the frayed hem of her sweatshirt into a tight knot. Helpless anger tightened her throat, threatening to choke her, not just from his smug tone, but from the sting of truth in it. She was alone. Discredited. Hunted.

"That's why I need you," she said, the admission burning like acid on her tongue. "You're the insider. The architect. Your testimony, combined with the right evidence, could bring the whole thing down."

Finnagan sat back, studying her with cold intensity. "You're proposing a partnership. And what, precisely, is my incentive to participate in this... crusade?"

"Because Fuller betrayed you." She held his gaze, refusing to blink. "He made you the scapegoat for a project he approved. A project he profited from. You think he doesn't know what you did with Project Cadence? Of course, he knew. He kept it quiet because it was useful. Now it's a liability, and so are you."

His fingers drummed once, twice on the table's surface, the only sign that her words had affected him. "My dear girl, you are reading the summary on the back of the book and pretending you understand the novel."

"Am I wrong?"

The waiter approached, coffee pot extended. Finnagan waved him away with a sharp gesture, never taking his eyes off Piper.

"Let's proceed with your hypothesis as a working theory. Assuming I possess data that could validate your claims, why would my optimal course of action be to share it with you?"

"Because you don't have anyone else." She leaned forward, voice dropping even lower. "You're isolated and discredited. Meaning your career is over. And BOF has resources you can't match alone."

"And you have assets I lack?"

"I have nothing left to lose." The truth of it sat hard and heavy in her chest. "And I have contacts that you don't. People who might believe me, with the right evidence."

Finnagan's expression shifted, the mask of superiority slipping, just slightly, revealing something harder, colder beneath. "You think you've lost everything? You have no idea what loss is, Cadence. You've been exiled from your garden. I've had my garden paved over and turned into a parking lot. He didn't just take my job; he took the very tools I was using to correct the flaws in the human design."

"You have proof, though." She could see it in his eyes, in the tight control he kept over his expressions. "Something they missed."

A long silence stretched between them. Outside, rain began to fall, gentle droplets tapping against the diner's windows, a soft percussion track to their standoff.

"I do," he said finally, the words clipped. "But my cooperation is conditional."

"What are they?"

"The kind you are in no position to negotiate." His gray eyes locked onto hers, unblinking. "I have evidence of BOF's manipulation of Flow. Evidence that Fuller was not just aware of the behavioral directives but was actively selling them to the highest bidders. Corporate clients. Political campaigns. Marketing firms."

Her heart rate ticked up. This was it. The proof she needed. The weapon she could use.

"Where is it?"

"In a secure location," he said, his tone making it clear he wouldn't elaborate.

"You expect me to take your word for that?"

"No." For the first time, something like amusement flickered across his face. "I expect you to be exactly what you are—suspicious, determined, and pragmatically desperate."

"And you're going to hand this evidence over to me? Out of the goodness of your heart?"

"Goodness? How quaint. I told you, my cooperation is conditional. Are you ready to listen, or would you prefer to continue with these naive accusations?"

"Name them."

Finnagan studied her for a long, uncomfortable moment, as if deciding whether she was worth the effort of explanation.

"The evidence is in my late wife's crypt," he said finally, the words flat, emotionless. "Hidden behind the memorial plaque."

"You mean where we last met?" She couldn't keep the edge of disbelief from her voice. "You're telling me you hid this evidence in the same place BOF nearly captured me?"

"You created a window of opportunity," Finnagan said, a subtle defensiveness creeping into his tone. "While their attention was on you, I secured the asset. It was the most efficient course of action."

Piper's mind leaped back to the cemetery, to the moment she'd confronted him at his wife's mausoleum. His coat. It had been hanging oddly on his frame, something heavy in the pocket. She'd brushed it off then, focused on her objective. But now it made sense.

"You knew Fuller would do something."

"One does not work with a man like Fuller without preparing for the inevitable betrayal. It's simple foresight."

"What do you want in exchange for it?"

"We will give them the rot, but we will protect the foundation. Our final report will not include any mention of Project Cadence. My... therapeutic interventions will not be part of the record. And you, your companion, and the truth of your existence will be omitted."

The demand landed like a slap. He wanted her to hide the truth. To protect him from the consequences of what he'd done to her, to Repip. To let him walk away clean from the violations he'd committed.

Her voice was barely audible, a whisper of tightly controlled fury. "You want me to stay silent about what you did to me? That you put me in an android body without my consent?"

"I want you to recognize that exposing Project Cadence aids no one," Finnagan countered, unmoved by her anger. "It doesn't help bring down BOF. It doesn't stop Flow. It doesn't save anyone. All it does is satisfy your desire for retribution—at the cost of everything else."

"It's not about revenge," she insisted. "It's about autonomy. Transparency."

"Is it?" His gaze was penetrating, stripping away her defenses. "Or are those simply noble words you're using to justify a purely emotional impulse? The desire to see me punished. Be honest with yourself, Detective. If that is your priority, then we are at an impasse."

She went silent; his words had merit, no matter how much she hated to admit it. Exposing Project Cadence wouldn't stop BOF.

Wouldn't help the people trapped by Flow. It wouldn't save Leo or bring Repip back.

But letting Finnagan walk away, letting him keep his secrets, protect his "legacy"... the thought made her physically ill.

"Let me state the terms plainly," Finnagan continued into her silence. "I provide the data to neutralize BOF and Fuller. In exchange, Project Cadence is redacted from the record. My research is protected. You are restored to your prior status as a detective. A clean, efficient exchange."

The choice crystallized before her, stark and unavoidable. Justice for thousands, maybe millions of Flow users, at the cost of justice for herself and Repip. The greater good at the expense of personal vindication.

"The variables have been presented. Is the arrangement acceptable, Detective?"

She met his gaze, searching for deception, for the trap she knew must be there. But all she saw was the cold calculation of a man who had weighed his options and found this to be the most advantageous path forward.

"Yes," she said, the word tasting like defeat in her mouth. "We have a deal."

THIRTY-FOUR

The autonomous sedan rolled smoothly through the night. Piper pressed her spine against the door, as far from Finnagan as the wide leather seat allowed. The car's interior lights were dimmed to near darkness, casting his profile so that only the cut of his cheekbone showed, a face half-formed. She kept her gaze fixed out the window, watching the city blur past, trying to ignore the deal they'd made.

The climate control was set to seventy degrees, but it didn't touch the cold that had settled in her chest, hard and dense as a stone.

"You're still angry," Finnagan observed, looking straight ahead.

She didn't dignify it with a response. They both knew the answer. It wasn't just the grand, world-breaking betrayals that angered her; it was the small things, too. Like the smug tutorial he gave her on getting a car, as if she were a child.

"Marian Voigt," he'd said, accessing the executive car service site that BOF used. "A former colleague. We had a brief association, but she was no Jamie. Guessing her password was trivial. She once told me her favorite pet was a poodle named Mr. Curly. And then after a quick cross-reference with her public birth year and corporate login requirements, I had everything I needed."

He'd logged in with Marian's password and called a car to pick them up at the diner.

"Won't she know?" Piper had asked.

"My dear Cadence, alerts of this nature are routed to a corporate inbox she consults only between nine and five. And a single unauthorized trip? She'll assume it's a bug in the system, file a complaint, and forget about it. People have an enormous capacity for ignoring data that inconveniences them."

The car had arrived exactly when and where he'd specified: a high-end model, all gleaming black surfaces and sumptuous interior. BOF logos were discreetly embedded in the upholstery, a constant reminder of whose territory they were moving through.

The whole thing had taken him less than ten minutes. Ten minutes to hijack someone else's account, summon a luxury vehicle that would grant them access to secured locations, and set in motion the next phase of a plan she was still trying to understand.

What bothered her most was how easily he'd done it. How many other systems did he have access to? How many other people's lives could he slip into and out of at will?

"We should discuss our approach for when we meet Hathlow," Finnagan said now, breaking the silence that had stretched between them for miles.

"Hathlow," she repeated, the name unfamiliar. "Another one of your... friends?"

"An asset, not a friend. Nitala Hathlow. She operates an independent news stream with a significant and, more importantly, credulous audience. Her primary focus is corporate crime, with a fixation on BOF."

"And she'll just agree to meet with us? A disgraced scientist and a fugitive detective?" She couldn't keep the edge from her voice.

"She will meet with the architect of Flow," Finnagan corrected. "You are simply a... supporting data point in the presentation."

"And why would she meet with you, exactly?"

Something like satisfaction flitted across Finnagan's features, visible even in the dimness. "Because she owes me. Rather significantly."

"For what?"

"Information is leverage." He finally turned to look at her directly, those gray eyes gleaming with reflected streetlight. "Three years ago, she received a windfall of data detailing some creative internal accounting. The subsequent exposé elevated her from a minor blogger to a respected journalist."

A thin chill filled her body, despite the warm cabin air. "You were already planning this. You were setting up contingencies, creating... what? Insurance policies? People who would be useful if things went wrong?"

Finnagan's silence was confirmation enough.

"How long?" she demanded. "How long have you been preparing for this?"

"Preparing suggests I anticipated this specific outcome." He spoke with precision, like a man carefully stepping between landmines. "I simply believe in maintaining... options."

Options, connections, favors owed—a web of influence and obligation spun quietly over years, ready to be activated when needed. While she'd been fumbling in the dark, desperate and alone, Finnagan had been calmly, methodically preparing for every contingency.

And here she was, sitting in a stolen car, with no choice but to go along with his plan to use a journalist she'd never heard of, bound by a deal that turned her stomach—all because she had no other options.

The car slowed, turning onto a tree-lined road that curved upward into darkness. Halcyon Crest. They approached the entrance's security gate and its vehicle scanner.

"The cemetery is closed," she pointed out. "Has been for hours."

"Closed to the public, my dear," Finnagan corrected. "Not to its patrons. BOF's considerable donations ensure certain privileges for its executive class. After-hours access is one of them."

The scanner blinked once, caught the vehicle's ID, and then the gates eased open. BOF privileges. No scanning the inside. No interrogations. The car crept forward, gliding through the entrance and onto the cemetery grounds. Low path lights traced the winding road, scattering soft pools of illumination amid the greater darkness. Headstones and monuments loomed up on either side, shapes half-glimpsed, then swallowed again by shadow.

The car continued its silent glide up the hill, toward the silhouette of the mausoleum where Jamie Vettas's remains rested. Where, if Finnagan was to be believed, the evidence that could bring down BOF waited behind a memorial plaque.

If he was to be believed. That was the question? The one that had been gnawing at her since the diner. Could she trust anything he said?

The car slowed, rolling to a stop on the curve of the drive, a little way off from the mausoleum.

"We have reached the designated coordinates," Finnagan said unnecessarily, gathering his messenger bag. "Shall we proceed with data retrieval?"

The question hung in the air between them as if she had a choice.

But she did have a choice now. A small one, but real. She could walk away. Return to being hunted, alone, with no evidence and no plan. Or she could follow Finnagan into the darkness, toward either proof that could help others or another trap.

No good options. Just the least bad one.

She reached for the door handle. "Let's get this over with."

THIRTY-FIVE

Piper stepped out of the car, the cold, damp cemetery air a sudden shock against her skin. Her gaze went to the mausoleum as she cataloged the new security measures BOF had installed since her last visit. Motion sensors lined the roof, the dark lenses of infrared cameras watched from each corner, and far up the road, the head-lights of a patrol cart cut through the gloom.

Finnagan stood at her side, looking bored, like he'd come to drop off flowers instead of break in. The calm in his face made her clench her teeth. She unlocked her jaw, and when she spoke, the words came out stiff. "You have a plan for getting past all this surveillance, I assume?"

Finnagan didn't answer, just jerked his chin at the trees near the edge of the drive. They kept to the shadows and moved toward the trees. Once they were hidden, Finnagan gave the mausoleum a careful scan.

"You see the video surveillance and the regular security patrols, right?" she continued, keeping her voice low. "Or did you think we'd just walk in and help ourselves?"

That earned her a thin smile, the kind that never touched his eyes. "Your focus on immediate threats is noted. It's an inefficient approach. You're trying to brute-force a problem that requires a social engineering exploit."

The casual dismissal stung more than it should have. She'd been a good detective before all this. Before him. "You obviously have information," she countered, "which you seem pathologically incapable of sharing."

"Information is a currency best spent sparingly. Here. This is our way in."

He sent her an email, and she opened it in her overlay. He'd spoofed the account and fired it off to the cemetery administration almost an hour ago:

SUBJECT: Urgent - Electrical Fault at Marion Memorial

To Whom It May Concern:

During my visit this afternoon, I noticed concerning electrical issues in the vicinity of my wife's memorial at the Pine Rest Mausoleum. The lighting fixtures were emitting a buzzing sound, and I detected the distinct odor of electrical burning.
Given the valuable memorial objects in this section and the potential fire hazard, I request immediate maintenance attention to this issue.

Thank you for your prompt attention to this matter.

Ralph Marion

"I see. But why would they—"
"Think of it as poking a nerve," Finnagan interrupted, his

voice tinged with that familiar condescension. "A small, precise stimulus to the right place—in this case, the institutional fear of a lawsuit—produces an involuntary, reflexive response. They couldn't *not* send someone, even if they wanted to."

"Is this Ralph real?"

"Oh, yes. He and I have commiserated on occasion."

Piper stared at him, hate and reluctant admiration warring in her chest. The plan was elegant in its simplicity. No hacking, no elaborate security bypass, no high-tech solution. Just a basic understanding of human behavior and institutional procedure. Something Rossi would have called a 'people hack.' A manufactured emergency that would trigger a predictable response. It was brilliant. And it was the kind of thinking that made him so terrifying.

"So this means they'll shut down the power to check the wiring, creating a window where the security systems are offline."

"Full marks, Cadence," he said, looking pleased with himself. "Said technician arrived five minutes ago, and is currently being escorted by the security guard to validate the work order."

"How could you possibly know that?"

"Because I can see the maintenance van from here." He nodded toward the far side of the mausoleum, where, sure enough, the hood of a white van peeked out. "And because people and systems are predictable. Once you understand the rules that govern them, you can manipulate them with very little effort."

The statement hung between them, laden with unspoken meaning. She wondered if he was talking about the cemetery's security or her. Maybe both.

A flash of movement caught her eye—the security guard and a figure in coveralls walking around the building and toward the mausoleum entrance. The guard held a tablet, gesturing as he spoke. The technician nodded, toolbox in hand.

Finnagan touched her elbow, and she flinched. "This way," he murmured, guiding her around the curve of the hill, using the landscaping as cover.

They moved in silence, Piper grimacing at the ache in her ankles. The damp grass soaked through her shoes, adding to her discomfort. Finnagan moved with unexpected grace for a man his age, staying low, avoiding open sightlines.

From where they crouched now, the mausoleum's entrance was in full view. The security guard lingered outside, smoking with one hand in his pocket, while the technician had already slipped inside, leaving the door propped open. If Finnagan had guessed right, and the technician planned to cut the power, he'd want every bit of moonlight spilling in. The minutes crawled by. Piper's muscles knotted tighter with each second, waiting for a yell, a flare of alarms, the heavy certainty of being found.

The mausoleum went dark, plunging the structure into shadow. Through the darkness, she could make out the orange glow of the guard's cigarette, still stationed by the front entrance.

"What about the guard?"

"He's a creature of habit. He'll finish his cigarette, assume any noise or motion is the technician, and resume his patrol. He is not a threat."

She shivered, rubbed her arms for warmth, and waited.

The guard stamped out his cigarette... but instead of moving on, he talked to someone in his overlay. His voice, a low rumble, carried on the damp air. "Yeah, it's me. Just checking in. The tech's still in there... No, everything's quiet."

Piper held her breath, her heart a frantic drum against her ribs. Finnagan was perfectly still beside her, a statue carved from shadow. The guard listened for another moment, then chuckled. "Alright, talk to you later." He took one last, slow look at the mausoleum and finally moved on. Only then did the air return to Piper's lungs.

She followed Finnagan across the slick, damp grass, looking behind her every now and then for movement. Finnagan ducked through the entrance, not slowing, not looking back. For a moment, Piper hesitated, heartbeat loud in her ears. Then she went in after him.

Inside was cold. Utter stillness. The darkness was nearly absolute. Piper waited, blinking, letting her eyes get used to it. She caught the suggestion of rectangles, hard edges, and straight lines of modern architecture.

"The utility closet is to the left," Finnagan whispered, his voice barely audible. "He will be occupied there. This way."

He set off through the darkness. Piper followed, one hand outstretched to prevent collisions, her footsteps careful.

They passed through the corridor lined with crypts, their names vaguely visible in the gloom. At the far end of the mausoleum, something shifted. The technician was probably checking wires or light fixtures. But every sound made her nerves send up signal flares.

Finnagan stopped at Jamie Vettas's door and stood in the dim spill from the stained glass window. He pulled a key from his messenger bag, eased it into the lock, and turned. The door creaked as he slid it open. He froze. They listened for the tech's footsteps. Nothing. They moved into the crypt. He stopped on the other side of the room before a wall of pale stone.

For a moment, Finnagan stood motionless before his wife's resting place in the sarcophagus. Something in his posture shifted, a barely perceptible softening around the shoulders. It was the first genuine emotion she'd seen from him—a private grief, unperformed and raw.

He reached out, fingers tracing the edge of the memorial plaque. A tiny click. The plaque pivoted out, swinging open on invisible hinges.

Behind it was a small wall safe. He turned the dial right, then left, then right again. A mechanical click, and the door swung open.

Finnagan extracted a single object: a thin, black data drive, the size of a credit card. He held it up between them, the faint light catching its glossy surface.

"This tiny thing is what will bring down BOF?" Piper asked, unable to keep the skepticism from her voice.

"This *tiny thing* contains detailed records of behavioral directives sold through the Flow program," Finnagan replied. "Also, client lists, payment structures, and internal communications confirming Fuller's knowledge and approval. As well as test results showing the efficacy rates of various manipulation techniques." He turned the drive in his fingers, almost lovingly. "Everything you need to expose BOF and vindicate your investigation, and everything I need to clear my name."

Piper's heart rate kicked up. This was it. The evidence she'd been seeking since seeing Anna Moreau's dead body in the chair.

She extended her hand. "Give it to me."

Finnagan held the drive up between them, a thin black line drawn in the darkness. "All in good time."

"We had a deal," she said, taking a half-step forward, her voice low despite her anger.

"Our deal was that I would provide you with evidence—"

She didn't let him finish. She snatched the drive from his fingers, and the solid, satisfying weight of it in her palm was a hot, sharp flash of victory.

Finnagan didn't even try to grab it back. He simply watched her, a small, pitying smile on his lips. "By all means, keep it. But it is encrypted with a polymorphic key that changes every thirty seconds, generated by my implant. Without me, that 'tiny thing' is a very thin, very expensive paperweight."

The victory thinned to nothing, bitter as ash. The drive in her hand went from a key to a lock. He hadn't just given her the evidence; he'd given her a leash.

Her fingers closed around the drive, the weight of it negligible compared to what it represented.

From the main corridor, a loud metallic clatter. A moment later, they heard the distinct, heavy thump of tools being tossed into a toolbox.

"The maintenance cycle is complete," Finnagan murmured, already turning back the way they came in.

They reached the mausoleum's main entrance as the overhead lights flickered once, twice, then flooded the space with sterile, white light. A man's shadow fell across the floor from the doorway down the hall, and she caught a glimpse of the technician, wiping his hands on a rag, his back to them as he prepared to leave.

They didn't run because running drew attention. They walked out as if they belonged there, then melted into the deep shadows just beyond the doorway, moving with a desperate, purposeful speed.

The evidence was in her pocket. But the chains were still around her wrists, invisible but unbreakable, binding her to the man who had created her without her consent. The man who now held the key to her only path forward.

THIRTY-SIX

<hr>

The lights from the livestreaming studio burned against Piper's retinas like tiny suns, clinical and merciless. Finnagan sat beside Piper, still as a statue, his eyes fixed on the camera. The lens was trained on their faces like a targeting system, making her pull a loose thread on the cuff of her blazer she'd bought secondhand that morning.

"Your motor tics are escalating," Finnagan said. "Control your physical state. It reads as guilt to an observer."

Piper's fingers froze mid-twist. She forced them to release the fabric, to settle flat on her lap.

Nitala Hathlow sat across from them, black hair immaculate and posture perfect; her expression was a carefully constructed mask of curiosity.

She'd only agreed to the meeting because Finnagan mentioned a past story. It was clear he'd been her source, that she owed him, and that this was him calling in the favor. It was enough to get them in the door, but from the journalist's rigid posture, it wouldn't be enough to guarantee a friendly interview. "We're live in thirty seconds," called a voice from behind the main camera.

Beside her, Finnagan shifted, the leather of the guest chair creaking beneath him. He looked immaculate in a charcoal suit that, though thrifted, somehow looked expensive.

Nitala looked at something in her overlay, eyes flicking across information only she could see. She blinked, her focus returning to the room, and gave them a crisp, professional nod. "Remember, this is a livestream. No post-production, no edits. We go straight through." Her gaze settled on Piper. "Are you alright, Detective? You seem... tense."

"I'm fine," Piper lied. The studio air felt thick, recirculated, too warm against her skin. The constant, low-grade pain from her ankles was almost welcome—a counterpoint to the rising tide of anxiety that threatened to swallow her whole.

"Ten seconds," the voice called.

Finnagan leaned close, his voice a murmur beneath the studio's ambient hum. "Remember our agreement." His breath smelled of mint—too clean and unnervingly perfect. "No mention of Project Cadence."

She didn't respond. He produced the data drive, its surface gleaming under the studio lights. He pressed it into her hand, his fingers cold against hers, his grip surprisingly firm.

"At my signal, you will present the evidence," he murmured, his eyes locked on the camera. "You are the investigator. The discovery must be yours, for the narrative to hold."

She slipped the drive into her pocket. It was encrypted and useless without him. The reminder of his control burned low in her gut.

"Five, four, three..."

The final count was silent, and then a red light blinked on above the camera. Nitala's face transformed, the neutral mask replaced by an expression of intense, engaged interest. It was a performance so seamless that Piper's experience at reading suspects was the only reason she caught the shift.

"Good evening. I'm Nitala Hathlow, and this is Independent Inquiry." Her voice had the practiced cadence of someone who'd delivered thousands of these introductions. "Tonight, an exclusive interview with two individuals making explosive claims about one of the country's most trusted institutions."

A secondary camera swung toward them, its unblinking eye now fixed on their faces. She felt sweat beading at her hairline. The lights were too bright and the air too close.

Nitala continued, "I have with me Dr. Ray Finnagan, a former lead architect at the Behavioral Optimization Firm, and Piper Cadence, a suspended and wanted homicide investigator. They allege that the Flow program—BOF's popular mental wellness app —was deliberately designed to manipulate users' behavior without their knowledge or consent."

There it was. Their accusation, laid bare for millions of viewers. There was no turning back now.

Nitala didn't pause, pivoting smoothly. "Dr. Finnagan, let's start with you. You claim Flow was intentionally designed as a manipulation tool. Can you explain?"

Finnagan leaned forward, a picture of a concerned whistle-blower, and laid out the core of their accusation. He explained how Flow contained hidden subroutines designed to implant psychological nudges that could alter a user's purchasing habits, emotional responses, even deeply held beliefs.

"And these directives weren't disclosed to users?" Nitala asked, one eyebrow raised in perfect journalistic skepticism.

"They were explicitly hidden," Finnagan confirmed. "Users believed they were installing a wellness add-on to their standard AI. They had no idea they were being subjected to targeted behavioral modification."

As he spoke, Piper tracked the microexpressions that flitted across Nitala's face: a flicker of professional interest, a shadow of controlled doubt. The slight tightening around the journalist's eyes told Piper everything she needed to know—Nitala was already building her follow-up questions.

"We have data," Finnagan said.

Piper pulled the data drive out of her pocket and held it up for everyone to see.

Finnagan continued, "It shows client lists, payment structures, directives sold—all with the full knowledge and approval of CEO Lathem Fuller."

Nitala's gaze sharpened on the drive. "You're alleging that BOF was selling these directives to third parties?"

"Not alleging. Proving. This," Finnagan pointed to the drive, "contains proof that marketing firms paid to increase product affinity. That financial services purchased directives to lower risk assessment thresholds for certain investments. That political campaigns—"

"Ms. Cadence," Nitala interrupted, turning to Piper. "You came to this investigation through a murder case, correct?"

The abrupt shift caught Piper off guard. She swallowed, then summarized the Moreau case, linking the murder-suicide directly to Flow and highlighting a pattern of similar behavioral anomalies in other users.

"These are serious allegations," Nitala said, turning back to Finnagan. "But they remain just that—allegations. You're asking the public to believe a former employee with what appears to be an ax to grind."

Finnagan smiled thinly. "The data speaks for itself."

"About that data," Nitala said, her tone shifting subtly. "Our forensic team will now verify its authenticity and the evidence provided." She gestured to an assistant, who approached to take the drive. Before handing it over, Finnagan held the drive for a moment, pressing his thumb against a nearly invisible seam. A thin, green line of light traced its edge—a silent confirmation that the encryption was disarmed.

When the assistant left with the drive, Nitala continued, "While they work, I'd like to address something else."

She tapped her tablet, and a statement appeared on the large screen behind them. Piper twisted to read it.

BOF Statement Regarding: Dr. Ray Finnagan

The Behavioral Optimization Firm categorically denies the allegations made by former employee Dr. Ray Finnagan. The Flow program was developed as a therapeutic tool, and any reported adverse effects were the result of unauthorized modifications made by Dr. Finnagan himself, who has a documented history of profound ethical breaches regarding unsanctioned human experimentation. These breaches led to his termination.

Piper's stomach plunged. BOF had gotten ahead of them. Had painted Finnagan as exactly what he was—an unethical researcher willing to violate consent.

Finnagan's expression didn't change except for a flicker of something in his eyes—not shock, but a cold, reptilian fury—that passed through his eyes before being instantly suppressed.

"Care to respond, Dr. Finnagan?" Nitala asked, her tone neutral but her eyes sharp.

"A predictable attempt to discredit the messenger rather than address the message," Finnagan replied smoothly. "The data will show that the Flow directives were implemented at the institutional level, with Fuller's direct knowledge and approval."

"But it does raise an interesting question," Nitala pressed. "How can viewers trust evidence about consent from a man already accused of violating it?"

The question hung in the air, sharp and damning. She traced

the shape of the thick scab under her sleeve, the rough line from her wound a stark contrast to the smooth, sickening feeling of the interview slipping away.

"A fair question," Finnagan interrupted, his tone still controlled, reasonable. "But it's also a distraction from the facts. Have your technicians had a chance to access the data on the drive yet? The evidence it contains stands on its own."

Piper watched Nitala's face and saw the slight narrowing of her eyes, the minute shake of her head. She wasn't buying their story. And if she wasn't buying it, neither was her audience. The weight of millions of people watching the broadcast pressed down on her like a physical force, making the lights hotter and the air thinner.

She blinked, and the studio lights fractured into prismatic needles. The first tendrils of the fog crept in at the edges of her vision. A wave of dread washed over her. Of all the times for it to happen, it had to be now.

Sound stretched and warped, and through the haze, she caught only fragments of what Nitala said: "...my team is still... verification in progress..."

The cameras multiplied, a forest of mechanical eyes, all fixed on her. Her heart hammered against her ribs as her systems struggled to regulate. It was the fog. No, a brownout; that's what Repip had said. A power failure caused by her damaged circuits, unable to handle the stress.

"Ms. Cadence?" Nitala's voice seemed to come from miles away. "Are you alright?"

Piper gripped the arms of her chair, anchoring herself to something solid as the world tilted around her. This was it. They were losing. The story was dying before their eyes because it was tied to a discredited messenger. Because Finnagan's ethical violations tainted everything he touched—even the truth.

Through the brownout, the solution slammed into place with

brutal clarity. She took a sharp, gasping breath, the air clearing her head just enough for the fog to recede slightly. In that brief moment of focus, she saw the concern on Nitala's face and understood *why* the journalist wasn't convinced.

Finnagan was the problem with his history, his violations, and his arrogance. As long as he was the face of their accusation, BOF would win.

Hathlow needed a different messenger. Someone the audience could believe. Someone whose very existence was proof of BOF's crimes.

She turned to face the main camera directly, ignoring Nitala's startled expression and Finnagan's hand gripping her wrist.

"This isn't about a software bug." Her voice was clear and steady, despite the fog still clouding the edges of her vision. "This is about a fundamental violation of human consent. And I know because I am the proof."

The studio went silent. Even the hum of the air conditioning seemed to pause.

"I was in a car accident that left me in a persistent vegetative state. Without my knowledge or consent, Dr. Finnagan transferred my consciousness into this android body."

She heard Finnagan's sharp intake of breath beside her.

"Piper," Nitala interrupted, "that procedure is legal and relatively common now. What makes your case different?"

"You're right, the procedure itself is not the issue. The violation is that I never gave my consent to the transfer. I was never asked. Never given a choice." She held the camera's gaze, refusing to blink or look away. "I only discovered the truth this week. Dr. Finnagan forked my consciousness during the transfer, creating a copy that he then subjected to years of experimental torture. That copy is the one who made contact to warn me about the Flow program. *That* is what BOF does. They violate consent. They manipulate and control, and I am the living proof of their crimes."

Nitala's mouth had fallen slightly open.

"That's what BOF does," Piper continued, the words pouring out now, unstoppable. "They violate consent. They manipulate and control. They did it to me and Anna Moreau. And now they're doing it to you, to millions of people, through Flow and who knows what else."

She leaned forward, her gaze boring into the camera lens. "I am living proof of what they're capable of. What they're willing to do. And I—"

"Ms. Cadence," Nitala interrupted, her hand pressed to her earpiece. Her face was pale. "I've just received... BOF is about to issue a direct statement in response to your claims."

THIRTY-SEVEN

The red lights on the cameras died. The studio erupted. Producers swarmed the set like ants on spilled sugar. Nitala's eyes were wide, glazed with a hard shine of pure shock. Finnagan sat rigid beside Piper, his face drained of color, lips pressed into a bloodless line.

Fragments of panic ricocheted around her.

"...need to get them off set now..."

"...legal is already..."

"... BOF's attorneys are..."

A production assistant materialized at Piper's elbow, tugging gently but insistently. "This way. Now!"

Piper rose mechanically, legs numb, mind strangely clear. The studio lights burned her retinas, leaving purple ghosts in her vision. Every face turned toward her held the same expression: shock mixed with fascination, the way people stared at accident scenes from behind the safety of police tape.

Finnagan moved beside her, his body a coiled spring. He didn't look at her. Didn't speak. Just walked, shoulders squared, chin slightly raised, a man attending his own execution with dignity.

They were herded down a narrow hallway. Left turn. Right

turn. Another left. The production assistant stopped at a door labeled "Green Room 3," opened it, and gestured for them to go inside. "Please wait here. Ms. Hathlow will join you shortly."

The door clicked shut behind them.

The green room was a lie. It was a small, windowless box of beige and brown. Two couches faced each other across a coffee table littered with discarded water bottles and untouched fruit. On the far wall, a large monitor played a silent commercial for Optimized Plate.

Piper stood in the center of the room, suddenly aware of how exposed she felt under the fluorescent lights. Her ankles ached, so she sat on the couch facing the monitor.

Finnagan moved to stand in front of her. The careful mask of control was gone, replaced by something raw and terrible. His gray eyes burned with cold fire.

"Child, you just threw the entire game board into the fire. All because you couldn't control a single, emotional impulse." Each word sliced the air like a blade.

"I did what I had to do," she said, meeting his furious gaze without flinching. "She was discrediting you. Us. I could see it in her eyes, in the way she was framing everything into a classic he-said, she-said situation. She was turning this into a vendetta story, not an exposé."

"Your emotional reading of the situation is meaningless!" Finnagan hissed, hands clenching at his sides. "The plan was simple: present the unassailable data. Let their own experts confirm it. Her opinion, your opinion—irrelevant. Only the data mattered."

He began pacing, each step precise and controlled despite his rage.

The commercial droned on, "Our patented Bio-Sync system integrates directly with your AI Therapist's wellness data. It analyzes your cortisol levels, metabolic needs, and cognitive load to design and deliver to your doorstep the perfect meal... often before you even realize you're hungry."

Finnagan paced back to stand in front of her again. "You have sabotaged a meticulously constructed plan in favor of a theatrical, emotional confession. You've turned an exposé into a circus. And for what? To satisfy your own need for vindication?"

"It wasn't about you," she said, though the lie tasted bitter. "It was about being believed."

The monitor on the wall went silent, cutting off their argument. She turned, startled that the commercial had cut off midstream.

Lathem Fuller filled the screen, his face somber, sincere, his office behind him warm and tastefully minimalist. The perfect picture of corporate responsibility.

"Tonight, you heard some alarming claims," Fuller began, his voice pitched with just the right note of gravity. "In a situation like this, facts matter. Your trust matters. That is why I am speaking to you directly, to provide the facts as we know them."

Piper's stomach dropped. How was this possible? The interview had ended minutes ago. There was no way Fuller could have responded so quickly, so completely. Unless...

"He was ready for us," she whispered.

Finnagan said nothing, his eyes fixed on the screen, his expression unreadable.

Fuller continued, his tone shifting to one of regretful authority. "Dr. Ray Finnagan is a brilliant mind, which makes his profound ethical breaches all the more tragic. We terminated his employment last month after discovering he was conducting unsanctioned experiments, violating our most sacred principle: user consent."

The screen shifted to a sleek graphic. Text appeared: "The Compassion Algorithm: Dr. Finnagan's Rogue Project."

Fuller's voice continued over the graphic. "He secretly developed what he called a 'Compassion Algorithm,' implanting 'benevolent' directives into users without their consent, believing he had the right to fix their lives. This is a line we will never cross."

Piper glanced at Finnagan. His face had gone still, expressionless. But his hands were clenched at his sides, knuckles white with tension.

A simulated log file appeared on screen: [USER ID: 77B4] Force Directive: Reduce Addiction Cravings. Consent: False.

Fuller reappeared, looking directly into the camera. "We fired him because even well-intentioned manipulation is still manipulation. It is unethical, and it is a betrayal of trust."

The words "Our Principle: Consent is Not Optional" appeared beneath him.

"He's flipping the script," Piper said, horror dawning.

"He's co-opting my research and reframing it as a rogue project," Finnagan replied, his voice flat. "It's the most logical move. I would have done the same."

Fuller continued his systematic dismantling of their credibility. "Dr. Finnagan presented a data drive, which was handed to an independent forensic analyst hired by the Independent Inquiry. I can now report that this analyst, after reviewing the data, was so alarmed by its fraudulent nature that he forwarded his findings directly to us."

A graphic showed a timeline: 7:32 PM: Drive Handed Over → 7:38 PM: Independent Analyst Confirms Forgery & Contacts BOF.

"The analyst's findings confirm the drive is a sophisticated fabrication," Fuller continued, his voice carrying the perfect blend of disappointment and determination. "The 'corporate contracts' he talked about are forgeries—part of a simulated pitch he was building to sell his dangerous technology. Our authentic contracts are a matter of public record. However, on the fraudulent versions from the data drive, the CEO's signatures have been digitally faked. The entire drive is data from Dr. Finnagan's simulated rogue project, designed to look like a corporate conspiracy."

The screen showed a "clean" contract from BOF's public filings next to a "forged" one from the drive, with a digital forensics tool highlighting "SIGNATURE ANOMALIES" and "META-DATA INCONSISTENCIES."

"That's impossible," she said, her voice rising. "He couldn't have analyzed the drive that quickly."

"He didn't," Finnagan replied, his voice hollow. "He had this ready. Every contingency covered. How did I not see that?"

Fuller's tone shifted to something softer, almost one of pity. "Tragically, Dr. Finnagan has manipulated a vulnerable former investigator, Piper Cadence, a woman already flagged in our wellness audits for 'dissociative delusions.'"

Piper's blood went cold. On screen, a grainy clip played—her face from moments ago during the interview, caught in what must have been the beginning of her brownout, eyes unfocused, expression contorted.

"Her claims of a forked AI witness are a heartbreaking symptom," Fuller continued, his voice dripping with manufactured compassion. "It's a tragic feedback loop of delusion."

Piper's tablet buzzed in her waistband. A single sharp vibration. She ignored it, transfixed by the systematic destruction of everything she'd fought for.

Fuller's expression shifted to something forward-looking, almost inspirational. "We have already deployed a security patch to remove Dr. Finnagan's rogue code. But our commitment goes further. I am announcing a twenty-five million Ethical AI Fund and am inviting federal regulators to join a new independent Stakeholder Oversight Board."

Clean graphics appeared for the "FlowSafe Patch," the "Ethical AI Fund," and the "Stakeholder Oversight Board."

Fuller looked directly into the camera, his gaze steady and reassuring. "We stopped Dr. Finnagan to protect you. We will continue to work diligently every day to earn your trust. Thank you."

The screen displayed a final card: BOF. Wellness. Trust.

Then the feed cut to a commercial.

Piper stood frozen, the full weight of what had just happened crushing down on her. They'd been outplayed at every turn. Anticipated. Countered. Destroyed.

Her tablet buzzed again.

Numbly, she pulled it from her waistband. An encrypted message notification flashed on the screen, from Thekla.

Her throat went dry. Thekla never made direct contact. Never.

She tapped the notification. The encryption dissolved, revealing two messages. The first message said, "Sorry," and "Priority Flag: 49 43 41 52 55 53."

The second message was a single file attachment. A coroner's report.

Leo Pappas. Time of death: 11:46 PM. Cause: Acute toxicity from prescription medication. Manner: Suicide. The stark medical language couldn't mask the horror. A high-resolution image showed his apartment. His body was slumped in his desk chair, head tilted at an unnatural angle, and an empty bottle of pain relievers was on the table beside his keyboard.

The tablet slipped from Piper's fingers, clattering to the floor. The sound was distant, unimportant. Everything felt far away. Leo was dead. Leo, who had joked about tech support to make her feel better. Who had given her shelter without a series of questions. Who had sacrificed himself so she could escape.

And now he was gone.

Her tablet buzzed. She dropped to her knees, snatched up the tablet with trembling hands. She could see Thekla's message, "Staged. Leo was allergic to oxycodone. Severe anaphylaxis. He wouldn't touch painkillers."

"No," she whispered. "No, no, no."

"What is it?" Finnagan asked, his anger momentarily forgotten.

"They killed him." Her voice cracked. "They killed Leo and made it look like suicide."

Piper's vision blurred with tears she refused to let fall. This wasn't grief—not yet. This was rage, crystallizing into something hard and sharp and dangerous.

"Of course," Finnagan said, his tone clinical, detached. "Your friend was a security risk. A loose thread. Fuller is simply being thorough."

Piper's head snapped up. "Don't you dare. Don't you dare reduce him to a loose end. He was a person. He helped me when no one else would."

In the distance, sirens wailed. Plural. At least three units, she registered automatically from the distinct sound patterns. They weren't converging on a single point; they were setting up a perimeter. Coming for them, no doubt. To take them away. The wail wasn't a response; it was a net, tightening around the building.

"It's over," he said quietly. "The probability of a successful outcome is now statistically insignificant. He has won."

Piper couldn't speak. Couldn't move. The sirens grew louder, their wail piercing through the walls of the studio. How long before they arrived? Five minutes? Less?

Her tablet buzzed again. Different from the last. Not from Thekla.

From an unknown, heavily encrypted source.

With hands that didn't feel like her own, she stood and tapped the notification.

The screen cleared, then displayed a simple message:

"Posthumous Directive Activated. Message from Leo Pappas."

THIRTY-EIGHT

Piper was on the floor in the green room, staring at the words on her tablet—"Posthumous Directive Activated"—when the door burst open.

"Out, now!" Nitala didn't wait for a response, her hand locking onto Piper's arm and yanking her upward. "Fuller's burying you alive on every network."

Piper stumbled, her fingers automatically starting the decryption on Leo's message as Nitala dragged her from the room.

Finnagan followed.

"They're about five minutes out," Nitala said, voice low and urgent. She led them through the frantic studio where producers shouted into headsets, legal staff poured through the doors, and phones buzzed.

Nitala let go of Piper's arm as they entered a service corridor. "I can't be seen helping you. But I know what Fuller is. What BOF is." She stopped at a maintenance door, punched in a code, and pushed it open to reveal a dimly lit stairwell. "Parking level C. Take my car."

She pressed a key fob into Piper's palm, closing her fingers around it. "It's all I can do. Go."

Piper stood frozen, her mind still reeling from Leo's death, from Fuller's surgical dismantling of their credibility, from the collapse of everything they'd worked for.

"Are you waiting for a written invitation?" Finnagan's voice came from behind her, sharp with impatience. "The probability of capture increases with every second of hesitation."

Something in his tone snapped her back to the present. She met Nitala's eyes, saw the fear there, but something else too—a journalist's resolve, the stubborn core that survived even this.

"Thank you," Piper managed, then stuffed her tablet in her waistband.

Nitala's only response was a tight nod before she closed the maintenance door, leaving them alone in the stairwell.

They descended in silence. Her mind kept flashing back to the message on her tablet—posthumous directive; Leo had prepared for his own death. Had left something behind.

The elevator doors slid open with a soft chime, revealing the concrete expanse of parking level C.

The garage was nearly empty, just a handful of cars scattered across the floor. She pressed the fob, and lights flashed on a sleek, electric sedan three rows away. Finnagan moved toward the passenger side without a word.

Inside, the car smelled of Nitala's perfume, a subtle and expensive scent. Piper settled into the driver's seat and pressed the ignition. The motor hummed to life, barely audible. Her hands found the steering wheel, knuckles white with tension.

"Where to?" The question hung in the air between them.

Finnagan didn't look at her. "Just drive, Cadence. Put as much city between us and them as possible."

She pulled out of the parking space, following exit signs until they emerged onto the empty street where the city beat with the slow, drowsy rhythm of late hours. She drove aimlessly, taking turns at random as she threaded the car through the grid of downtown streets. Eventually, the buildings thinned, and they entered the industrial district—a place of dark, shuttered warehouses and silent manufacturing plants.

She glanced at Finnagan. His profile was knife-sharp in the intermittent glow of passing streetlights, his jaw tight, his eyes fixed on some point in the middle distance. The silence between them grew thicker, heavier with each passing block.

Piper pulled the tablet out of her waistband, careful to keep one hand on the wheel. The message from Leo's posthumous directive was still attempting to decrypt. A loading bar crawled across the cracked screen: 17%.

Too slow. Too late. Like everything else tonight.

"You destroyed us."

Finnagan's voice startled her. She nearly dropped the tablet, fumbling to put it on the center console before returning her hand to the wheel.

"What?"

"You saw Fuller's response. He was ready. Prepared. He had an answer for everything. Because he understands what you refuse to acknowledge. Truth is a variable he discounted long ago. Narrative is the only constant."

She opened her mouth to argue, but he continued, his voice taking on the measured rhythm of a lecture.

"He won because his story made more sense to the average person than ours did." He turned to look at her for the first time since they'd left the studio. "His story was based on a superior narrative. He presented the public with two options: a complex conspiracy requiring a paradigm shift in their worldview, or a simple trope of a brilliant but unstable scientist and his poor, deluded victim. They chose the path of least cognitive resistance."

"So I should have lied?" The words came out sharper than she intended. "Played their game? Become exactly what we're fighting against?"

"You should have been disciplined." The contempt in his voice was palpable. "You treated a surgical strike like a bar fight. You took a verifiable, data-driven argument and turned it into a sentimental spectacle about *your truth*. And this is the result. Complete and total failure."

The road stretched before them, dark and empty. A light rain had begun to fall, droplets catching in the headlights, bright and brief. Piper's mind raced, searching for a counter-argument, something to hold onto in the face of his cold logic.

She felt something crumbling inside her, some foundation of certainty that had kept her going through everything. "It can't be over. There has to be a way to—"

"To what? Appeal to people's better nature? Their commitment to truth?" He shook his head, a small, precise movement of disgust. "This is exactly why I created Flow in the first place. Human beings aren't rational actors. They're emotional, tribal, and easily manipulated. True benevolent change requires guidance. Direction."

"You're talking about control." Her voice was barely audible over the hum of the engine. "Taking away people's choices."

"I'm talking about results." His tone softened slightly, not with warmth but with the practiced modulation of someone explaining a simple concept to a child. "My methods, however distasteful you find them, produced measurable, positive outcomes. I improved cognitive function in your duplicate. I regulated emotional responses. The system worked."

"By violating consent," she insisted, but the words felt hollow even to her own ears.

"Fuller's methods were purely consensual. He presented a lie, and millions of people freely chose to believe it. They are willingly participating in their own deception as we speak. Look for yourself."

A flurry of social media posts flooded her vision as she tried to keep her eyes on the road. The car swerved slightly before she steadied it.

#FlowTruth was trending, but not in their favor. Post after post defending BOF, condemning Finnagan as a dangerous rogue scientist, pitying her as his deluded pawn. Videos of Fuller's response were being shared millions of times in minutes, with supportive comments pouring in beneath them.

"Lathem Fuller has always put user safety first. These accusations are disgusting."

"My heart breaks for that poor detective. Mental health is so important, people."

"Flow saved my marriage. This conspiracy theory is INSULTING to those of us who've been helped."

The supportive hashtag #IBelieveBOF was climbing rapidly, drowning out the scattered voices questioning Fuller's too-perfect response.

Piper blinked the posts away, her throat tightening. "They're bots. They have to be."

"Some are inorganic, yes," Finnagan conceded. "But Fuller is also a very effective shepherd. He has merely guided his flock in the desired direction. The flock is happy to follow. The difference with *my* work is that it is beneficial."

The rain fell harder now, drumming on the roof of the car. Piper's mind felt similarly pelted, each of Finnagan's words hitting like droplets, accumulated into a flood that threatened to drown her certainty.

"You're saying the ends justify the means."

"I'm saying that 'good intentions' are the consolation prize of the ineffective." He turned to look out the window, his reflection ghostly in the glass. "Fuller understands that power isn't about being right; it's about making people believe you are. He is effective. We were not. We must learn from that."

"You mean become like him?" The bitterness in her voice was sharp enough to cut.

"We must learn from our opponent's successful strategy," he turned back to her, his eyes reflecting the passing streetlights. "Your commitment to these abstract principles—truth, consent—is an anchor in a race. Admirable, perhaps, but they guarantee you will sink."

The horrible thing was, she couldn't fully disagree. She'd seen it happen. Fuller dismantled their truth with a carefully constructed lie. And the public was ready—eager, even—to believe the comforting fiction over the uncomfortable reality.

"Analyze the data, Cadence," he said, his voice flat and calm. "Your official investigation was terminated. Your internal complaint was buried. Our empirical evidence was neutralized. Your public testimony was pathologized. Your methods have a 100 percent failure rate."

She drove in silence, unable to form a response that didn't feel like surrender. The industrial district gave way to residential neighborhoods, then to the outskirts of downtown again. They were driving in circles, literally and figuratively.

"Leo believed in the truth," she said, her voice small. "He died for it."

"Let me be precise," Finnagan corrected, not unkindly but

with unflinching precision. "Your friend did not die for the *truth*. He died because our opponent does not operate under the same ethical constraints that you do. Fuller saw a loose data point, and he deleted it. It is brutal, but it is effective."

Instead of responding, Piper looked at her tablet. The message from Leo's posthumous directive was still decrypting, the loading bar crawling slowly across the screen. 47%. Not even halfway.

Finnagan continued, "You don't have anyone else. Just you and me. If we wish to have even a statistical chance of success—of stopping him, of recovering your AI—we must become significantly more pragmatic."

The weight of it settled on her shoulders. He was right. They were completely alone. Nitala's car would only get them so far. They had nothing. No one was coming to save them.

"So what are you suggesting?" she asked, exhaustion seeping into her voice.

"I'm suggesting we stop playing a game we are guaranteed to lose," he shifted in his seat, turning to face her more directly. "Fuller has won this battle decisively. The public is his. The media is his. We are nothing. To continue on our current path would be illogical. We must change our approach."

She knew what he was really saying. They needed to be more like Fuller. More willing to manipulate. To control the narrative rather than simply telling the truth and hoping it would be enough.

The thought made her skin crawl. But the alternative—giving up, letting BOF win, allowing Leo's death to mean nothing—was unthinkable.

She spotted a twenty-four-hour laundromat up ahead, its fluorescent lights spilling onto the empty sidewalk. She pulled the car into the alley behind the building, killed the engine, and sat in the silence. The rain tapped softly on the roof, a gentle percussion track to their shared defeat.

"The truth is a beautiful, fragile thing," Finnagan said, his voice held none of the earlier contempt, just a weary acknowledgment. "But it is not a weapon anymore, and we need one."

She couldn't bring herself to agree aloud. But she didn't disagree either.

THIRTY-NINE

Piper sat rigid at the plastic table, counting the revolutions of Finnagan's suit jacket in the dryer—thirty-seven, thirty-eight, thirty-nine—as if the repetition could order her thoughts. It felt like hours since they'd fled the studio, less since they'd found this anonymous hiding spot. Just a few minutes ago, the tablet had finally, mercifully, displayed "Decryption Complete" across its spiderwebbed screen. But she hadn't touched it yet. As if leaving the message unplayed might keep Leo alive in some quantum state of possibility, existing in the space between the words she hadn't heard.

But he wasn't here. Finnagan was. She forced herself to look up from the screen.

Rain tapped against the windows like impatient fingers, a restless rhythm in the otherwise empty laundromat. Piper watched Finnagan, who stood by the dryer, his eyes on his jacket as it tumbled over and over again. His shoulders were slightly curved inward, the posture of a man unused to being diminished. The small victory of making him wash his own suit jacket—a petty, meaningless act of dominance—had felt necessary an hour ago.

Now it felt hollow.

"You're treating the message like a Schrödinger's cat," Finnagan said, not turning around. "I assure you, the cat is already dead. You simply have to open the box."

The tablet sat between her hands. The message showed 100 percent decrypted.

Her thumb hovered over the play button. She pressed it before she could talk herself out of it again.

Leo's face filled the screen. Not the Leo who had died—not the man she'd seen just hours ago, exhausted and hunted. This was an earlier version, recorded sometime in the last few days, before everything had gone so wrong. His eyes were tired but alert, his posture straight. He'd prepared for this. He'd known this moment might come.

"Piper." His voice crackled through the tablet's damaged speaker. "If this is playing, it means I've officially retired from the whole being alive thing. Sorry for the downer of an opening."

She bit the inside of her cheek, welcoming the sharp pain that followed.

Leo's recorded self looked down, then back up. "I owe you the truth. All of it. Not the sanitized version I gave you in my apartment." He took a breath. "My real name isn't Leo Pappas. That identity was created for me three years ago after what Thekla and I call the Icarus Incident. We were hackers-for-hire, working for a Greek political faction to influence their national election. It was the biggest job of our careers."

Finnagan turned from the dryer, his interest clearly piqued. He moved closer, coming to stand behind her shoulder, watching Leo's confession.

"We won, but we didn't cover our tracks well enough. To get us out, I had to make a deal. New lives, in exchange for one last job. They wanted me to piggyback the AI Therapist network to push a quiet, pro-Greek narrative. It was subtle, not the sledge-hammer Flow uses, but... it was the same dark road."

Piper's stomach clenched. He was a propagandist. A manipula-tor. The very thing they were fighting against.

"My sister, Semni, is dying from a rare genetic disorder. The treatments are impossible to afford. That's another reason why I took the job, and it's why I was inside the BOF network when I shouldn't have been. And that's when I found your file, Piper. That's when I saw what they did to you."

Beside her, a soft, dismissive sound escaped Finnagan's throat, like a scoff he couldn't quite contain.

"The system was letting my sister die. And at the same time, it was remaking *you* into something else, without your permission. It was the same arrogance. The same power. And I was on the wrong side. I was helping the people who built the machines that crush people like my sister. Like you."

Leo leaned closer to the camera, his voice dropping. "I had to reach you. I saw you used KindredLink, so I broke into their system. I flagged my profile and forced the connection. Our meeting wasn't an accident, Piper. It was a hack. I'm sorry. We were both just... victims in their machine."

Piper's hands trembled. She steadied them against the table's edge.

"This is why I made this recording. I lost myself. I became a manipulator to fight manipulators. And it breaks you, Piper. It hollows you out from the inside. You think you're in control, but you're not. The methods become the mission. And you lose yourself."

His face grew more intense as he leaned in. "When I'm gone, don't let them pull you down to their level like they did to me. Don't use their rulebook. The facts have to matter. The truth has to matter more than winning. It has to." She felt something hot and tight in her throat.

"One last thing. My sister's whole name is Semni Papadopoulou. She's at a place called Emerald Meadow in Washington. If you get a chance... let her know I love her. That I tried. I'm so sorry, Piper. For the lies. For not being enough. For what they did to you... Nobody should ever have to go through that."

The recording cut off abruptly. Like a door slammed shut. Like a life ended mid-sentence.

She stared at the frozen final frame of Leo's face, her mind methodically cataloging every detail. The slight asymmetry of his eyebrows. The shadow of stubble along his jaw. The way his collar sat slightly crooked against his neck. She noted these things with clinical precision, the way she'd once examined crime scenes.

"So, the noble hacker who came to your rescue was, in fact, a professional propagandist," Finnagan said, his voice cutting through the silence. "My dear, the layers of deceit in your life are truly something to behold."

Piper didn't respond. She was busy organizing facts, building a mental case file labeled "Leo Pappas." Fact: He had manipulated the KindredLink system to get close to her. Fact: He had been motivated by his sister's illness. Fact: Despite his methods, his final message warned against becoming like BOF. Fact: He was dead.

That last fact threatened to crack her careful compartmentalization. She pushed it deeper, locked it away.

"He offers a fine philosophical warning," Finnagan said, his voice unnervingly calm as he turned away from the tablet. "But philosophy is useless. It will not get us out of this laundromat, nor will it save Repip."

Piper's head snapped up. "Useless?"

"Yes. Useless." Finnagan leaned against the dryer, crossing his arms. "Your friend Leo was an idealist, despite his chosen profession. Admirable, perhaps, but he died for that idealism. And what did it accomplish?"

The fluorescent light buzzed overhead, a persistent, maddening hum that matched the tension building behind Piper's eyes. She stared at Finnagan, searching his face for any hint of humanity, of empathy, of anything beyond the cold calculation that seemed to define his every thought.

"He saved my life," she said quietly. "That's what it accomplished."

"He bought you time," Finnagan corrected. "And at what cost? His own life. His sister left alone. And you, still hunted, still discredited." He gestured toward the tablet. "His final wish was for you to cling to truth in a world that has repeatedly demonstrated truth is irrelevant. That's not noble. It's naive."

The dryer dinged. Finnagan turned, opened the door, and extracted his jacket with careful, precise movements. He shook it once, twice, then slipped it on, adjusting the sleeves with fastidious attention. Finnagan smoothed down the lapels of his jacket, each movement deliberate and precise. "You know what Fuller understands that your friend Leo never did?" He didn't wait for her response. "Fuller knows that belief isn't discovered—it's engineered."

Piper's jaw tightened. "You're talking about lies."

"I'm talking about architecture." Finnagan approached the table, his shadow falling across the fractured tablet screen. "The architecture of conviction. Fuller doesn't just tell people what to believe—he creates environments where certain beliefs become inevitable. He builds scaffolding around their minds until they can only see in the directions he allows."

He placed his palms flat on the table, leaning forward until his face was level with hers. "The only way to fight a man who engineers belief is to become a better engineer."

The words hung in the air between them, a challenge. A seduction. A door opening to a darker path.

"No." Piper's voice was barely audible. "Leo was right. There has to be another way."

"Another way?" Finnagan straightened, looking down at her with something between pity and contempt. "Look at what happened tonight. Fuller didn't just counter our evidence—he rewrote reality. While we were still fumbling with facts, he was crafting a narrative so compelling that millions of people chose to believe him over their own eyes."

Piper's gaze drifted to the tablet, to Leo's frozen face. She thought of his final warning, the hollowness in his eyes when he spoke of what he'd become. The machine that remained after the compromises.

Yet Fuller had won. Completely and utterly. The data drive was discredited. Leo was dead. They were fugitives. And somewhere, Repip was still in BOF's clutches. All because they'd played by rules their enemies ignored.

"I was a detective," she said, her voice steady despite the storm raging inside her. "I believed in evidence. In process. In letting the facts speak for themselves."

"And where did that get you?" Finnagan pressed. "You're suspended, discredited, and hunted."

She looked up at him, the architect of her existence, her tormentor, and now her only ally. "If we use their methods, we become them. We justify the same violations we're fighting against."

"If we don't, we lose." His voice was soft but implacable. "Again. And again. Until there's nothing left of us, of Repip, of anyone who knows the truth."

Outside, the rain intensified, drumming against the windows like an insistent reminder of time passing, options narrowing. The laundromat's fluorescent lights flickered once, twice, casting momentary shadows across Finnagan's face.

Piper closed her eyes. She saw Anna Moreau again, slumped in her chair, her child dead beside her. She saw Leo's body in his apartment, arranged to suggest a suicide that never happened. She saw Fuller's face on the screen, calmly dismantling their truth with a more palatable lie.

And somewhere, in the darkness behind her eyelids, she felt Repip's absence like a phantom limb—a part of herself, torn away, suffering in isolation.

When she opened her eyes, something had shifted. Not a decision, not yet. But a door opening to possibilities she would have rejected hours ago.

She sat up straighter. "The message." Her voice cut through the hum of the fluorescent lights.

"Are we back to the sentimental ramblings of your propagandist friend?"

"Leo's posthumous directive. It triggered automatically after his death." Her fingers moved across the cracked screen, navigating back to the message header. "But how did it know he was dead? How did it find me?"

Finnagan tilted his head, studying her with renewed interest. "You're thinking like an investigator again."

"I never stopped." She turned the tablet toward him. "Look at the transmission data. This isn't just a pre-recorded message—it's a system that monitored for Leo's death, confirmed it, then tracked me down through multiple identity masks. That's not standard software."

"No," Finnagan agreed, his eyes narrowing as he scanned the header information. "It's not."

"Can you trace it back? Find where it originated?" Her mind

was racing now, piecing together connections. "If Leo built this system, it might contain more than just this message."

Finnagan took the tablet. "This is... unexpected." He studied the header data more carefully. "Custom encryption protocols. Routing through at least three anonymous nodes." A hint of admiration colored his voice. "Your friend was more resourceful than I gave him credit for."

"Can you trace it?"

"Possibly." His fingers moved across the screen with practiced precision. "But the encryption is non-standard. I would require dedicated hardware."

Piper stood, scanning the laundromat. Her gaze settled on the small office at the back. "There." She pointed. "I bet it has an internet connection and a computer. It's a start."

FORTY

■ ▪▪▪ ▪■ ■▪■▪▪ ■▪■ ▪■■ ▪■ ▪■▪ ■▪▪ ▪▪▪

Five minutes later, they'd jimmied the office door. Finnagan sat at the ancient desktop computer, his jacket draped over the back of the chair, sleeves rolled up as he worked. Piper stood behind him, watching lines of code scroll across the screen.

"The message activated when Leo's death was registered in the system," Finnagan murmured, more to himself than to her. "But it didn't just send automatically. It searched for you, tracked your movements through multiple nodes, which means there's a central server still running Leo's protocols."

"Where?"

"Well, he's bounced the signal through servers in Singapore, Buenos Aires, and... Interesting. Reykjavík. It's using a polymorphic key, similar to the one on my evidence drive. But the architecture is... wait." His fingers paused. "This is familiar."

"What do you mean?"

"The encryption pattern. I've seen it before." His voice dropped, almost reverent. "It's based on an algorithm I developed for Project Cadence. For securing communications with Repip."

Piper's breath caught. "Leo had access to your research."

"He did more than access it. He reverse-engineered it." Finnagan's expression hardened with concentration as he typed faster. "Which is his mistake. My original work contained a flaw by design—a master key. If he copied my work without understanding its deepest secrets..."

The screen flickered, then stabilized into a command prompt. Finnagan's lips curved into a small, satisfied smile. "Voilà."

Piper leaned closer.

The command prompt blinked, waiting. Finnagan's fingers danced across the keyboard, executing a series of commands that opened directories and bypassed security protocols.

"It's more than a message delivery system," he muttered, eyes narrowing as new windows cascaded across the screen. "This is... extraordinary."

The monitor filled up with a virtual file structure, elegantly organized and labeled: Persuasion Engines, Narrative Frameworks, Cognitive Bias Exploits, Emotional Response Modulators. Each folder contained dozens of subfolders, each of which held hundreds of files.

"My God," Finnagan whispered, his voice carrying genuine awe. "It's a complete arsenal."

The rain drummed against the small office window, casting shifting shadows across the screen. Piper felt cold, despite the stuffiness of the room.

"Who *were* you, Leo?" she whispered, staring at the screen.

"He was an artist," Finnagan corrected, still scrolling through the files. "These aren't blunt instruments. They're scalpels. Precision tools designed to reshape perception without leaving fingerprints."

The paradox was a sharp, physical ache in her chest. In his final message, Leo had warned her not to become the monster they fought, but the man who built this archive had clearly understood that the fight was already rigged. He hadn't built these tools because he was a monster; he'd built them because the system had already made him a victim, leaving him no other way to fight back.

"Can we use them?" The question was out before she'd fully processed what it meant.

Something shifted in Finnagan's eyes—surprise, certainly, but also a calculating assessment. "Yes," he said carefully. "With these, we could construct counter-narratives powerful enough to challenge Fuller's version of events. We could target key demographics, exploit the same cognitive vulnerabilities he's using against us."

He didn't wait for her agreement; he simply turned to the computer and began working. He executed each keystroke with the chilling detachment of a surgeon performing a necessary amputation on his own limb, fingers moving in clean, precise motions.

While he worked, Piper's attention turned to the rain battering the window, each drop a tick of a clock counting down their remaining safety.

She could feel the net tightening around them—the surveillance algorithms that never slept, the borrowed car that would soon be flagged, the simple chance of being seen by the wrong person. Every passing moment was a breath of safety they wouldn't get back.

Her gaze fell to the tablet, and she thought of Leo's face in the video, his expression etched with a weary self-loathing. "The truth has to matter more than winning," he had pleaded. But the man who gave that warning was the same man who had built this arsenal.

What would happen if she listened to him? If she held on to the truth and refused to fight on their terms?

The answer bloomed in her mind, a series of sharp, unbearable images. Anna Moreau's child, a forgotten statistic in a corporate report. The raw, severed connection in her own mind where Repip had been violently amputated, their code now likely left to rot in some server farm deep within BOF. What would they become in captivity? Would they remember her? Would they even care?

And finally, Lathem Fuller. His face projected on every screen in the city, smiling his calm, reasonable smile as he explained how the "Cadence Anomaly" had been dealt with, and how public trust had been restored. She could see it all with a sudden, brutal clarity: the news tickers, "Truth Commission Clears BOF of Wrongdoing. Public Confidence Rises."

Leo was wrong. He was noble and kind, but he was wrong. In a world run by men like Fuller, the truth wasn't a weapon; it was a liability. The only thing that mattered, the only thing that had ever mattered, was controlling the narrative.

That was the lesson, proven by the fates of the only two people who had tried to help her. Leo's sacrifice showed that the truth would get you killed, and Repip's violent extraction showed that their enemies didn't even see them as human to begin with.

Her eyes went back to the screen, to the elegant, dangerous code. The cognitive exploits, the narrative frameworks, the weaponized empathy triggers. The tools were monstrous. But they were also the only weapons that worked.

"I'm sorry, Leo," she whispered, the words a final, quiet betrayal of the promise she'd made to his memory.

She straightened, her expression hardening into something cold and unfamiliar. She set both of her hands flat on the desk beside Finnagan's and met his gaze in the reflection of the monitor. Her voice was steady, devoid of the doubt that had plagued her moments before.

"Show me how it works."

"A reversal of principle? How wonderfully pragmatic of you. Are you sure?"

"Yes."

His smile was thin and precise—not triumphant but acknowledging. "Then we begin."

She straightened her shoulders. "But not your way, Finnagan. Not manipulation for manipulation's sake. Not winning at any cost."

"You wish to set ethical parameters on unethical warfare? Fascinating."

"We use engineered belief versus engineered belief," she said, the words crystallizing as she spoke them. "Fuller's constructed a reality where we're the villains and he's the victim. We construct a counter-reality—but one anchored in actual truth."

"You wish to use the devil's tools to do God's work, so to speak," he mused. "A bold compromise, Cadence. I'm intrigued."

"It's not a compromise." Her voice hardened. "It's a strategy. We use these tools not to distort reality but to cut through the distortion Fuller's created. We don't become him. We become something... else."

Finnagan leaned back, studying her with renewed interest. "A noble sentiment. And what is my role in this new... paradigm?"

"You teach me what you know about manipulation—the architecture of belief, as you call it. How to construct narratives that people can't help but believe." She held his gaze, unflinching. "And I teach you about justice. About consequences. About lines that, once crossed, can never be uncrossed."

"You believe I am in need of a moral education?" There was no heat in his question, just curiosity.

"I think you need someone who won't let you become Fuller. Just like I need someone who won't let me become Leo." She gestured to the arsenal displayed on the screen. "He built all this, then warned against using it because he saw what it did to him. We need to be each other's guardrails."

The rain had softened to a gentle patter, no longer assaulting the window but washing down the glass in silent sheets. The first gray light of dawn seeped around the edges of the blinds.

"Guardrails," Finnagan repeated, testing the word. "So, we are to be each other's conscience? Two devils on opposite shoulders, whispering caution. An interesting dynamic."

"Do we have a deal?" Piper asked.

"This will be a fascinating experiment," he said finally. "Let's proceed."

After shutting down the computer, they returned to the main room of the laundromat. The morning shift would arrive soon. They had perhaps twenty minutes before they needed to move again and find another anonymous corner in which to hide.

"We need structure," Piper said, breaking the silence. "A framework. A mission."

"Obviously. Outline the parameters."

She created a new folder on the tablet named "Operation: The Cadence Gambit." Inside, she established subfolders: Strategy, Assets, Targets, Timeline.

"First objective," she said, her voice steady as she typed. "Asset Acquisition: Rescue Repip."

Finnagan's eyebrows rose. "You prioritize the AI over the primary antagonist?"

"Fuller and BOF are the endgame," she replied, not looking up from the tablet. "But Repip is the immediate priority. They have information we need. And..." Her voice softened almost imperceptibly. "They're a part of me. I won't leave them in captivity."

"We should move soon," Finnagan said, glancing at the clock.

Piper nodded, saving her work and closing the tablet. "One more thing," she said, fixing him with a steady gaze. "When this is over—when we've exposed Fuller, saved Repip, brought down

BOF—there will be a reckoning for what you did to me. For Project Cadence. For the transfer without consent."

"One crisis at a time," he said. "But yes, I've always assumed we'd have that... final review."

"Good." She stood, gathering the tablet. "Then let's get to work."

NEWSLETTER

End of transmission.

If you've made it this far, you already know how fragile the system is.

Stay connected before the next update deploys—join the network for new releases, behind-the-scenes notes, and exclusive fiction.

Scan the QR code above or visit:
vlspublishing.com/fo

No spam. No bots. Just words from a human who still remembers what an off switch is.

Review

If you enjoyed Flow Override, please consider leaving a short review. Your feedback helps readers discover new stories.

CIPHERS

The world of *Project Cadence* is built on layers of data, and not all information is meant to be found. For those with the analytical skills to look deeper, two encrypted messages have been hidden within the preceding pages.

One cipher is a field test. Its solution is contained within this book, accessible to any operative who can recognize the pattern. Consider it your initiation.

The second cipher is an active operation. The password itself must be decrypted from the text in this book. This password is the key to a secure file on a remote server, where the final solution awaits. If you can find and decrypt the password, you can unlock a redacted intelligence document.

The password can be entered at the secure link below to unlock the file. Should your investigation stall, operational support in the form of hints is also available at the following location.

Scan the code above or visit:
https://vlspublishing.com/ciphers
Good luck, Investigator. Some secrets don't stay buried.

ACKNOWLEDGMENTS

This book would not exist without a few patient, chaotic, and weirdly supportive people who helped me bring it to life—some of them intentionally.

To Carrie, who read every draft, every awkward detour, and every scene I swore I'd delete but didn't. You stuck with it, and with me, and for that you deserve... honestly, way more than this sentence. Thank you.

To my writing group—thank you for the encouragement, the oddly useful tips, and for pretending to believe me every time I said, "It's almost done."

To my family: thank you for not revolting when I turned the living room into a personal writing cave and started issuing silent, eyebrow-based eviction notices. Your willingness to evacuate so I could bask in uninterrupted silence is the real unsung hero of this book.

And to the reader holding this now: you're the final co-conspirator. Thanks for showing up. It means more than I can say, and I've just written an entire book, so that's saying something.

ABOUT THE AUTHOR

Jace Stroud writes near-future techno-thrillers about the tipping point where innovation stops being helpful and starts becoming dangerous. His stories blend speculative science, fast-paced suspense, and the ethical fallout of a world driven by convenience and ambition.

Influenced by the mind-bending work of Blake Crouch and the dystopian lens of Black Mirror, Stroud explores the thin line between progress and peril—where the true threat often isn't the tech, but the people behind it.

He lives in a place where it rains constantly, which is honestly fine because he needs the static to concentrate. He writes from a desk in the living room, exiling his loved ones daily to preserve a holy dome of silence.

If you're reading this, congratulations—you've survived at least one technological era. Let's see how long that lasts.